RED, RED, WHITE
A NOVEL OF TRUE LOVE AND LIGHT
Evie's journey continues

....

VICTORIA WRIGHT

Will & Mato

Thank you for always believing in me.

Table of Contents

CHAPTER 1 — THEIR STORY

When I turned the key, the lock clicked, and I felt a surge of nervous energy enter my body. I lifted the lid, finding everything so neat and organized. It was as if they wanted to tell me their story.

I slid the locker to the middle of the floor and leaned against the couch, remembering how overwhelmed I was the first time I had opened it. This time would be different. I knew my mother, what she did, and why they kept her work secret from me. Now it was time for me to learn about my grandparents, Lilly and Peter Prince.

Under the stack of my mother's postcards was a leather-bound photo album. I slowly opened the cover. Front and center were my grandparents on their wedding day. She looked gorgeous, and he looked so young. I slipped the photo from its holder and turned it over—1953. My grandfather twenty years old, and my grandmother eighteen. A beautiful couple who looked so happy.

Slowly flipping through the pages, I observed their early life together. Travel and adventure. Their life looked amazing.

A bundle of postcards spilled from the album.

Dearest Lilly,

We arrived safe and sound. The village is in worst shape than we thought. They definitely need our help. I expect I will be here for a month, maybe two. I will write again soon.

Stay strong and know that I dream about your beautiful face every night when I close my eyes.

Your loyal husband,

Peter

"What? My grandfather did humanitarian work? How could that be? He hated that my mother did the same thing."

I skimmed through a few more postcards. Bolivia. Chile. He had traveled throughout South America, helping people. That made little sense.

Putting the postcards down, I leaned back on the couch, closed my eyes, and took a few deep breaths. My mother did the same thing as him. Why was it so wrong for her? Was it because she was a *woman*? My mind raced. How sexist. No wonder my grandfather was so strict with me. *Ego, just stop*, I said to myself. This was their life, their decisions. I couldn't be mad.

Hold up. *Yes, I can*, because their decisions had affected me. I felt like I was on a seesaw—my emotions up and down, openness and allowing, and then anger and judgment.

Further into the album, I found a photo of my grandparents in front of this house. They had dated it "*1959. Our forever home.*" The remaining photos depicted a storybook life. Pictures of my grandparents and my mother. My grandfather at the boatyard. My grandmother painting. Life seemed incredibly joyful for them. My grandfather actually smiled in the pictures.

I closed the album then got up to make myself a cup of coffee when something shiny caught my eye. I reached into the locker and pulled out a pocketknife. Simple but sturdy. There was an inscription. I couldn't read it, so I took it over to the window to get a better look. "'*Share your light.*' What does that mean?"

As the coffee brewed, I gazed out the kitchen window. So much I didn't know … So many things that I had no control over that had molded me into who I had become.

My eyes welled with tears. What had happened that made my grandfather such a different person with me? He had been so happy and carefree. What had changed him to become so critical and protective? Was it me? Was it my fault?

I moved out to the deck to drink my coffee while listening to the hum of the cicadas. It was going to be a warm one.

After a brief meditation, I grabbed my phone. *Hmm … Tatum emailed me.*

> *Evie,*
>
> *Hope you are well. I have an interesting proposition for you. One of my long-time buyers is interested in your work and would like to commission a piece. He is offering ten thousand dollars and needs it by the end of October. They will hang this in the entryway of his newest hotel in Bali. Great exposure!! If you are interested, I will send you the details.*
>
> *Look forward to hearing from you.*
> *Tatum*

My giggle started off quiet and low but quickly turned into hysterical laughter. I couldn't catch my breath, which caused me to snort and wheeze.

"Hey, what's going on over there?" Granddad yells through the bushes.

I finally catch my breath and answer, "This is unbelievable. Someone wants to commission a painting from *me*!"

"Congratulations, kid. That is fantastic news. Hey, I'm heading out. Need anything from down island?"

"Nope, I'm good."

"Okay. I'll be back later this afternoon and want to hear all about this opportunity."

I plopped down on one of the deck chairs, my legs shaking. To control myself, I ended up pacing back and forth.

OMG, can I really do this? Just thinking about painting on demand made me break out in a cold sweat. I took a deep breath and decided to talk with Tatum before I got too weirded out.

She didn't answer.

"Sorry I missed your call. Please leave a message at the tone."

"Hey, Tatum. Just got your email. This is amazing. But, to be honest, I am nervous. Can we talk? Please call me."

My phone rang just as I walked back into the house.

"Tatum, thanks for calling back so quickly."

"Of course. Incredible opportunity, right?"

"Yes. To be honest, when I read your email, all I could do was laugh. Someone really wants to commission my art?"

"Mmhmm … So, let me give you some background. As I mentioned, he is a long-time client of mine who I have placed art in most of his hotels around the world. However, this is the first time he has asked to commission a piece. Well-respected and very willing to promote the people he works with. Grand opening is on November 5th, so he will need it before then. Don't worry about framing or shipping. He and I will do all of that. All you need to do is paint."

"But, what kind of painting? Anything that comes to mind?"

"He really likes your moody pieces. The lobby color scheme is very modern, so he would like more dark, saturated colors."

I got immediately into the minutia and said under my breath, "I may need to order the canvas, as I don't even know where I can buy canvasses on the island."

"Ha! So, you gonna do it?"

I gave a long pause. "Yes," I whispered.

"Great. I will send you all the information that you need, including pictures of the lobby. This is a turning point in your career, Evie. This can really launch you. Talk with you soon."

"Uh-huh."

Tatum hung up, and I listened to the silence. *What have I done?*

I walked around the house, room to room, talking to myself. "I can do this. It's just painting, and I love painting. But this is different. So big. So much money. He can make or break me."

I stopped pacing and found myself in the middle of my grandparents' room. I dropped onto the bed and said in a low voice, "Grandma, I wish you were here to help me."

In the back of my mind, I heard, "*So talk with her.*"

"Can I do that?" I asked out loud.

"*Yes. Protect yourself, and I will help you connect with her.*"

***

To clear my head, I needed to walk. The fog hadn't completely burned off, so the beach-goers wouldn't be out yet.

The morning was quiet as I walked along the road without fear of being hit. There were no sidewalks up island, so everyone shared the two-lane road, including cars, cyclists, and pedestrians. My walking partners this morning included a rabbit and a wayward skunk that I gave a wide breadth to.

A spectacular scene of pure beauty emerged as the fog slowly lifted, and the blue sky appeared. The lighthouse was in the not too far distance, and I could barely see her calming light beams—two reds and a white. She always gave me a sense of belonging. That light had gotten me through many lonely nights, missing my mother. I didn't have to think about anything as the lights just lulled me into a calm trance.

Built in 1799, the light served as a beacon for wayward sailors, warning them of impending danger from the rocky waters. After fifty-plus years, she had been moved from the cliff's edge, rebuilt out of brick, and given a new light. Due to continual erosion, she had made her final move from the cliff's edge one hundred and seventy some years later.

A short, dirt road led me to the park that surrounded the lighthouse. Lush, green grass, boarded by a weathered fence, an ocean view backdrop that would gob-stop even the most hardened person.

The lighthouse was red brick. She looked weathered, but her presence was strong. It was apparent that she would be around for many more years to come.

I sat down on the ground with my back against her, closed my eyes, and entered my meditation. The brick was cool, and I felt her strength and energy. My meditation was short, but it allowed me to calm my mind and to think about how I would approach this new opportunity. I didn't want to open the door to my grandmother yet. This one was all me.

Then I walked the short, dirt path, which led me back to the road that encircled the historical park area. A set of steps led up to the shops and the viewing area of the clay cliffs. The area had become full of activity, with tourists milling about, going into stores and taking pictures. The view of the cliffs never got old. Some days, all you could see was the white, black, yellow, and grey clay. Other days, you might see a little red amongst the other colors. Whenever the water was red, a deep sadness would fill me, as it was proof that the cliffs were washing away with each wave that broke upon the shore.

Before leaving, I walked into one shop to buy Hendrix a T-shirt. I had no idea what size he was, so I held each one up and tried to measure how I fit within the arm area of the shirt, pretending that I was snuggled into him.

A woman approached me. "Hi, can I help you?"

"Yes, do you have this T-shirt in a 2XL?"

"Give me a sec and let me see what I have in the back."

When she returned, she handed me a T-shirt. "Here you go."

"Thank you." I gave her my credit card.

She read my name on the card then gave me another look. "Didn't you go to high school here?"

"Yes, I did, but for only a couple of years."

"I knew it! You looked really familiar. I'm Celeste. We were a few years apart. How long are you here for?"

"Hi, Celeste. I am embarrassed, since I don't remember many people from that time."

"No worries. I know it was a long time ago. I remember you kept to yourself a lot."

"Yes, those were a couple of tough years for me. I had just lost my mother; that is why I was here, living with my grandparents."

"Oh, I am so sorry. I didn't know."

"Please, don't worry. I didn't tell many people. But enough of that, you asked how long I am here for. Actually, I just moved back from Denver a few months ago. I bought my grandparents' house, so I am just down the street."

"Really? That is great. What do you do?"

"I'm a painter. So, I moved my business here to the island."

"How exciting!"

"Do you own this shop?"

"No, I just work here to make extra money in the summer. I have a full-time job working at a bakery down island. My schedule there is only four days a week, so I pick up other work where I can, to make ends meet."

She handed me back my card and placed the T-shirt in a bag. "Are you showing at any of the galleries?"

"No, but I hope to one day."

"Personally, if I was an artist, I would have my own gallery, but I am a bit of a control freak. I see people do it all the time around here. Have it opened when it suits them. Everything on their own terms."

Celeste's comments made me think.

"Maybe one day …" I dreamily replied then told her, "Celeste, it was so nice to meet you. What bakery do you work at?"

"Bread & Spice"

"OMG, I love that place! The ham and cheese croissants are to die for. Good thing I don't go down island often, or I would be huge."

"I am so glad you like them. Those are my specialty."

"You made them?" I squealed.

Celeste blushed and nodded her head. "I work primarily on weekends up here during the summer, so stop by again to say hi."

"I will. Have a great day."

Unfortunately, the walk home was less relaxing. The sun was out, it was hot, and it seemed like the world was rushing to get to the beach. Overall, though, this morning's outing was a good one. Made a new friend, and her idea of starting my own gallery really intrigued me.

I wanted to share my news with Hendrix, but first, I texted a picture of me wearing his new T-shirt with the caption "*All for you.*" This should wake him up.

As I expected, my phone rang soon thereafter.

"Good morning, beautiful."

"Good morning. You wouldn't believe what happened to me this morning." Before he could say anything else, I launched into telling him about the new painting opportunity and meeting Celeste.

"Wow, you have been busy. How do you feel about the commissioned work?"

"I am trying not to freak out. Excited, but it feels like this buyer could make or break me."

"Evie, stop. Please don't think that way. You are putting too much pressure on yourself. When someone commissions artwork, they trust the artist. They love what the artist has done in the past and know they will love what the artist will create for them. Have confidence and trust yourself."

I paused to take in his words before responding, "Thank you. I needed that."

"Anytime. So, are you sending me that shirt, or do I have to come and get it?" he asked mischievously.

I giggled and stammered. He always got me so flustered.

I took a deep breath. "It will be waiting when you decide to come and get it."

"My hope is that it will be really soon. I gotta go now. I love you, Evie Prince."

I blushed, even though he couldn't see me. Oh, how I wanted to say those words back to him.

"And I know you love me, too, so no need to say it." He chuckled.

I sheepishly responded, "I will call you later. Can I get a hug before you go?"

"Coming right at ya."

His energy filled my body.

"Mmm … that felt so good," I purred. "Have a great day."

When we hung up, I felt like I was floating.

I don't know if this is love, but whatever it is, it feels wonderful, I thought to myself.

***

Outside, I watched a hawk soar through the sky, and a pang of sadness hit me, knowing that some unsuspecting rabbit or mouse would soon meet their demise. Envy also crept in. To fly and to see the beauty of life all around would be awesome.

When the hawk flew from my sight, I began noticing all the things that I still needed to do around the house—re-shell the driveway, fix the holes in the road, clear some more of the land. The list continued to get longer. With each new to-do, I could feel the anxiety rising within me. Then, out of the corner of my eye, I saw something flit by. A bright green hummingbird. Amazingly beautiful. Chirping as it gathered nectar.

Who knew hummingbirds chirped?

Excitement filled me, but I was cautious, so as not to frighten the hummingbird. I wanted this moment to last.

Whatever anxiety I had flew away with the excitement of seeing the hummingbird. A smile crossed my face, and I heard Granddad in my head say, *"Just listen to nature. It will tell you all you need to know."*

What is nature telling me today? I wondered. Granddad would know.

The beauty of the hummingbird gave me my inspiration for the day. I set my easel up on the deck, my favorite spot, closed my eyes, and relived the emotion I had felt at seeing the hummingbird.

The warmth of the sun on my face, and a little kid's excitement at seeing such natural beauty. Shimmering greens, dark blues, a blur of the wings, yet the precision of the beak. Abstract and clarity all at the same time.

Hours passed. When I finished, my face was red and completely sunburned by the midday sun. On the canvas, for all to see and feel, was the energy of the hummingbird.

I stepped back and admired my work. *This is a good one*, I proudly acknowledged.

To celebrate, I went inside, opened the fridge, and grabbed myself a beer. *It's 5:00 somewhere*, I thought to myself as I rummaged around, finding the last one behind the container of orange juice.

Filling my mouth with beer, I enjoyed letting the cold liquid run down my throat. The cold bottle relieved my sunburned cheeks, too, reducing the heat, if only for a few minutes.

Looking out the kitchen window, I saw Granddad slipping through the bushes, heading toward the house, so I met him outside.

"Beer already? Guess it's been a hard morning."

"Actually, it's been an amazing morning. I met someone who I went to high school with, saw a skunk and a rabbit on my morning walk, watched a hawk, and experienced the energy and beauty of a hummingbird. On top of all of that, I painted. Want to see?"

Granddad whistled. "Nature had a lot to say to you today," he commented as we walked around to the deck, where I dramatically revealed my painting.

"Ta-da!"

"Oh, kid, this is a good one."

"Right? I love how I captured the green shimmer of the breast feathers, and the energy just gives me goosebumps."

"No wonder someone wants to commission your work," he complimented. "So, tell me all about this opportunity."

We took a seat, and I gave him the details, but I knew he could tell that I was holding back.

"Sounds absolutely amazing, but what is really going on?" he probed.

It immediately transported me back to high school. Granddad could always get me to tell the real story, no matter how much I resisted.

"I'm nervous," I blurted out. "Wonder if he doesn't like it?"

"If he doesn't, then he doesn't. There is not much you can do about that. He knows what he is doing. Commissioning work comes with unknowns, but he trusts your work enough to know you will create beauty. Just paint, and everything will be perfect. Kid, *you* manifested this opportunity. Now just allow it to be and enjoy the ride."

"None of this surprises you, does it?"

"Evie, there are no surprises in life. It is all created," he replied.

We both sat there for a few moments, thinking about what we had just discussed.

I broke the silence. "Granddad, can I ask you something … about the hummingbird?"

"Sure, what about it?"

"You've said that nature tells all. What was the hummingbird telling me today?"

Granddad closed his eyes, and I could tell he was gathering his thoughts. "Nature was giving you many messages today. Let's start with the hawk. The hawk is a messenger. It is asking you to be aware of the signals in your life. The hawk sees all. Open your eyes and see all that is around you."

I go into deep thought about what Granddad just said.

"Did you say that you also saw a skunk?"

"Oh, yeah."

"The skunk commands great respect. Through its reputation, people and animals alike understand to give the skunk a wide berth. The skunk asks that you notice how you are projecting yourself. What type of energy are you putting out there? Just like a skunk, who is small in stature, but can chase away a predator ten times its size, it asks you to be confident in yourself. Now, the rabbit … The rabbit symbolizes fear. The more you speak of your fears, the more you bring them to you. Rabbit is reminding you to stop the what-ifs and release your fear. Finally, the hummingbird. This beautiful, little bird represents the love of life and pure joy. It asks that you stop being judgmental and to relax. She brings energy and beauty. She is reminding you to enjoy life."

When Granddad finished, I was absolutely stunned and sat in silence, trying to process all that he said.

"What's wrong, kid?"

"You weren't kidding that nature knows all. So many lessons …"

"Evie, these are reminders. You know these things. Nature is *reminding* you of what you already know. Now it is up to you to follow."

CHAPTER 2 — WHAT IS LOVE

Well, if I am going to paint this masterpiece—I laughed to myself—*I need a canvas.*

Tatum had already sent the dimensions, lobby pictures, and color scheme. Trying to think this through, however, I realized that I had never painted something so large. So, not only did I need to get the canvas, but I also needed to find a surface large enough to paint on.

Not knowing where to look, I fell back on what I knew. Therefore, I called the art supply store in Denver to see if they could source and ship me the size of canvas that I needed.

"Mile High Art Supply, this is Shiloh. How can I help you?"

"Shiloh, my name is Evie." I said in a friendly tone. "You probably don't remember me, but you helped me several months ago purchase painting supplies. I asked you about getting over the fear of not selling your paintings, and you provided some brilliant advice."

"Oh yeah! I remember you. How can I help?"

"Well, I no longer live in Denver, but I am hoping you can help me source a large canvas—seventy-two by thirty-six-inches. I've been commissioned to do a piece but have never painted something so large."

"Congratulations! I guess the concern about not selling your paintings is a moot point now," she responded with a chuckle.

"We can definitely get you a canvas that size. Give me your email and where we need to send it, and I will price it out for you."

"Thank you. I live on an island now, and this is not something that I can purchase easily."

"An island?"

"Yes, Martha's Vineyard."

"Oh, nice. No worries. I should have the information for you tomorrow."

"Perfect."

After hanging up, I let out a tremendous sigh of relief. *One step closer*, I thought to myself.

***

Outside was warm and inviting as I walked down the stairs and sat on the bottom step to think about how I was going to pull this off. My paintings resulted from my emotions. I had no connection to this hotel, no feelings toward the man who would purchase the painting, and was completely unsure of what he expected of me.

Looking down, I noticed an ant carrying a small piece of food. "Hey, where are you going, Mr. Ant?" I asked out loud.

The ant's tenacity to bring the food back to his ant hill made me wonder, *What would happen if I put a stone in your way? Would you climb over it or go around? Or would you try to push the stone out of your way? You are strong for such a little guy.*

The ant made me reflect on my own life. I was the type to push obstacles out of my way, believing going around it was weak. But, sitting here now, I realized that my beliefs had changed. This ant was not weak if it went around. It was just another path, another point of view, a different way of doing things.

To complete this painting, I knew I needed to see and do things differently.

Immediately, I visualized myself as a skunk—tail up high, confident, and aware of my capabilities.

"I'm no stinking rabbit," I said in my best gangster voice.

There are no more what-ifs. I could do this.

***

The dirt road got the best of me today. I misjudged and hit a hole, nearly knocking my muffler off the car.

"Shit! I knew this would happen!" I yelled.

When I got out of the car, the muffler was hanging by a thread. I left the car and walked back to the house.

Rummaging through the junk drawer, I found some wire. Unsure of exactly how I was going to do this, I secured the muffler until it could get fixed.

That was it! I needed to get this road fixed.

In the garden shed was the shovel. With great determination, I stomped back down the road and identified the culprit hole.

The packed dirt made it difficult to break up. Every time I lifted the shovel, I kept thinking, *I will not be one of those women who needs to hire a man to do things for her. I am not weak.* My agitation grew with each shovel full of dirt.

Two holes, that was it, and I was already exhausted. A late afternoon swim was what I needed to give myself a break.

The tide was almost out, and there was a beautiful sandbar glowing in the water. I waded out farther and farther until I reached the soft, yellow sandbar. It was about thirty feet from the shore, but the water was only ankle deep. The waves were small and crested in multiple direction, creating a swirling dance. I plopped right down in the middle and let the waves dance around me. The water put me into a melodic trance.

Time passed unnoticed. The tide had risen, and it startled me to realize what was originally ankle-deep water had risen to knee-deep. Looking back to shore, I saw I was the only one left on the beach, and no longer could I wade back; I had to swim.

Swimming was not my friend, even though I had taken lessons as a kid, and then again as an adult. It was the breathing part—face in and out of the water—that always wigged me out. Floating on my back and doing the backstroke was okay, but putting my face in the water and doing the crawl for a long distance flat-out scared me.

I walked to the end of the sandbar and looked back at shore. This would be the longest distance I had ever swum. It was getting dark, too, so I needed to get back quickly.

The sandbar dropped off, and I did a makeshift breaststroke, keeping my face above water. I was getting nowhere fast, so I switched to the crawl. My swimming instructor's voice filled my head, "*Cup your hands and use long, powerful strokes.*" Better, but I was getting tired.

Panic set in, and I started flailing around. I knew I needed to relax, but I couldn't. Not only was I scared of drowning, but the dark water freaked me out even more. Anything that touched my legs made me frantic.

Evie, breathe. Calm down. You can do this, I repeated in my head.

It didn't work. My head went under.

I kicked frantically and somehow bobbed back to the surface, but I couldn't stay there long. I didn't know what to do. I was screaming in my head, *Swim! Swim!* but my arms and legs were too tired from trying to fix the holes in the road. They gave out, and my body slipped under again. I struggled to come back up.

Then I heard, clear as day, just as if someone was whispering in my ear, "*Float. Stop fighting and float.*"

A surge of energy entered my body. I rose to the surface and laid my head back into a dead man's float. An absolute stillness came over me. My breathing slowed, and I became calm. Then, slowly, I kicked my legs and reached my arms back over my head. Left then right, each stroke pulled the water like a rope, closer and closer to shore. I looked up into the dusky sky and said, "Thank you."

The rest of the swim was a blur. Finally, I stumbled out of the water and fell onto the sand, completely exhausted but somehow at peace.

When I got home, I went directly to the outside shower and allowed the warm water to wash the evening away. The stars shone brightly, glittering in the dark night sky. I thought of the ant with the crumb and the wisdom that Colbie had given me months ago. Life was not supposed to be hard. I needed to stop fighting. When I surrendered and listened to my heart, I could overcome my fear.

The shower calmed me, and when I opened the stall door, I stepped into what seemed like a firefly celebration. Little flashing lights, on and off, dancing all around and filling me with hope.

Magical.

***

The next day, I could barely get out of bed. My exhaustion lingered, and my arms and legs were as heavy as cement. Knowing that I couldn't fix the road by myself, I went over to Granddad's, seeing if he could recommend someone who I could hire to help me.

"So, what exactly do you need?" Granddad asked.

"I am looking for someone to help me fix the holes in my road. Oh, and I need a place to hang a seventy-two by thirty-six-inch canvas."

"Hmm … summertime is hard, kid. Everyone is working like crazy. You could probably ask Steve. I don't know if you remember him. He came to the house when I was being taken to the hospital. He's a volunteer firefighter and EMS, but he does carpentry work as his day job. You can find him most late afternoons over at the firehouse."

"Great. I'll stop by there tonight after I drop off my movies at the library."

How life had changed. Libraries were always beautiful, ornate buildings that looked good in the movies, but I never thought about going into one. Living on an island, libraries were the lifeblood of the community. Going to one felt like a social outing. Similar to the dump, you could always find out what was going on in town, and the movie selection was as good as any movie service.

On the way back to the house, I heard my phone ringing and rushed inside, grabbing it just in time.

"Hello?"

"Hi, Evie."

"Hi. Who is this?"

"Hey, it is Sue, your old next-door neighbor."

"Sue? How are you doing? So nice to hear from you," I replied, trying to remove the shock from my voice.

"Thanks for taking my call. I was hoping to chat with you about something that I'm thinking about doing. Do you have time?" she asked shyly.

"Sure. What's going on?"

"Before you left, do you remember me telling you I had always wanted to be a florist?"

"Yes."

"After you moved, I took your words to heart, and I started thinking about what steps I could take to eventually become one. A few online floral design classes gave me the courage to engage with my favorite florist. Based on your advice, I offered to do some pro bono accounting work, and they jumped at the offer. I have been helping them for the past month."

"Sue, that is amazing news. How do you feel?"

"I feel fantastic. It is definitely extra work, but it feels like I am doing something for me, something that I enjoy."

"That is wonderful. So, you mentioned you were thinking about doing …"

"Well, they offered me a stake in their florist business."

"What? That is amazing!"

"You would think so, but I don't know what to do. I mean, I would really like to do it, but it's an enormous investment. The pandemic has put a lot of pressure on small businesses, and …" she stammered.

"You're scared," I stated.

"Yes, I'm scared," she admitted.

"So, you are scared. It's okay to be scared. Let me ask you this. If you were to walk away tomorrow from this opportunity, would you be able to sleep at night? Would you miss being around flowers?"

"Oh, I would definitely miss being around flowers. To be honest, I probably wouldn't be able to sleep."

"Seems to me you found your answer."

"But, what if it fails?"

"Then you take those lessons and move on. When I moved to the island to paint, I had just interviewed for my dream job. Then I thought about the amount of work it would take to succeed and how I wouldn't have time to paint, and I realized I wouldn't be happy. Now that I have found happiness, I can't deny myself anymore. Who knows if I will be successful? But, if I'm not, then there is always something else that I can do. Like I said to you before, I would rather take a chance on me than rely on my company to take care of me."

"Evie, I believe that I have found my happiness," Sue announced.

"Congratulations! Sometimes that can be the hardest part. Do you trust yourself?"

"Yes."

"Well then, if you trust yourself, and it feels right to you, then take the leap. Stop listening to your ego. It will limit you and tell you what cannot be done. Listen to your heart, and everything opens up, and somehow, what you desire, what brings you happiness, will be."

I heard faint sobbing, and then a long pause.

"Evie, thank you. I have been so unhappy, and I didn't know how to change. When I saw you turn your life around, and you were so confident, I was jealous but needed to know how you did it. I wish we had spent more time together when you were here, in Denver. I know I could have learned a lot from you."

"Sue, I was no different from you for most of the time I was in Denver. This awakening and belief in myself are new. I learn every day, and please don't think this is easy for me. I fall back into old patterns easily. But, what is different is that I can now recognize those patterns that do not serve me and can pivot and change my perspective and attitude. Once I do that, things open up and wonderful happens."

"So much to learn."

"No, so much to *remember*. You know how to do this—we all do—but we have been conditioned to forget. Remember, beliefs are just that—something that you have been told and you believe. If you choose to believe something else, you have the freedom to do so. Choose to believe in you. Choose to believe in your own happiness. Doing that will raise your energy, and you will attract more of the same."

"Evie, I can't thank you enough for your help. May I call again?"

"Of course. And, remember to listen to your heart. That is something that I have to remind myself of every day."

"I will try. Oh, I was so caught up with me that I forgot to ask: How is the painting going?"

"A lot has happened since I moved back, but I am about to start a piece that someone has commissioned."

"What? That is fantastic!" she screamed. "I guess it can be done, and you are living proof."

"Yes, I guess I am," I replied with a chuckle.

We said our goodbyes after that.

The joy I felt from helping someone find their own happiness erased the pain I felt in my arms and legs. No wonder Colbie did healing work. It felt so good.

It was getting late, and I realized I needed to get over to the library and the firehouse.

I gingerly maneuvered my way down the road, as if the car was tiptoeing to avoid as many bumps and holes as it could. The muffler didn't fall off, but you could hear me coming a mile away.

The library was busy, as usual. Summer people sat outside on the steps and in their cars, tapping into the library's Wi-Fi.

The library was an old, one-room schoolhouse, with red-painted shingles and white trim. It had been a library since as far back as I could remember, but back in the day, it had been a school that had served the children of the local indigenous tribe.

I strolled in, said my hellos to the ladies at the desk, and returned my movies.

I overheard a few people quietly discussing the topics of the upcoming selectmen's meeting. Politics were not my thing, so I made a beeline for the movie section to grab my weeks' worth of evening entertainment.

On the way back to the desk, I noticed a flyer advertising a gallery showing next weekend.

"Hmm … Maybe I should check that out?" I said under my breath.

Barbra, the librarian, noticed my selection of movies. "Into sci-fi, huh?"

"Thought I'd try something new. Don't you ever wonder what else is out there?" I replied in a spooky voice.

"Nope. Whatever it is out there, it can stay there. I am not interested in meeting some alien being, unless he is cute, of course. It's hard to find a good man on this island," she said with a big grin.

I smiled back.

"You'll see. Winters on the island are night and day to the summers, especially if you live up island. Not as much to do and not as many people. Some may like it, but personally, I find it a bit too quiet."

"Actually, I look forward to some downtime. Plus, it will give me more time to paint."

"Oh, you will have plenty of time to paint," Barbra commented as she checked out my movies.

We said our goodbyes then I walked over to the firehouse. It was a two-story, brick building, just big enough to house one firetruck and another emergency vehicle. The building was well-kept, and it looked like a fresh coat of paint had just been put on the trim.

I walked around, trying to figure out how to get in, when I heard, "Can I help you?"

I couldn't see where the voice was coming from, so I simply stood there, looking around.

"Hello, can I help you?" I heard again. "Up here."

I took a step back and looked up. From the second-story window, I saw a man looking down at me.

"Hi, I'm Evie Prince, and I am looking for Steve."

"Well, you found him. What can I do for you?"

"My granddad, Attaquin Brown, suggested I speak with you about some work that I need done at my house."

"Attaquin is your granddad?" he replied with a puzzled look.

"Yes, it's a long story."

"Sorry, don't mean to get into your business. I didn't know Attaquin still had family. And when I met you at his house, you didn't say he was your granddad. I thought you were living in your grandparents' house."

"I am. As I said, it's a long story."

He changed the subject and asked, "What kind of work do you need done?"

"My road is a landmine of holes, and I was hoping to get someone to fill those in. Also, I need a wooden structure that can hold a large canvas for a painting that I will start soon."

"Hey, you're an artist?"

"Yes, I am," I stated. *Oh, how far I have come*, I thought to myself. Not too long ago, I would have been too shy to say that I was an artist. Now I could say it with pride.

"Cool. My cousin is also an artist. She is actually having a showing this weekend."

"Wow, congratulations to her." I didn't admit that I had seen the flyer in the library.

"Well, I can't commit to anything until I see what I'm up against. How about I stop by tomorrow before work?"

"Great. Thank you. My road is the one just before Granddad's," I said before turning and walking back toward the library and getting in my car. Instead of going straight home, I took the scenic route and drove by the beach. The waves were gigantic. My windows were down, so the sound of the crashing waves against the beach, then the dragging rocks back into the ocean, created a hypnotic song.

I pulled off to the side of the road, turned off the car, and just listened for a while. Sometimes, at night, if I really listened, I could hear the ocean music back at the house.

The smell of the salt water and the crashing of the waves completely relaxed me. My mind wandered, and I thought about Hendrix, who I hadn't heard from since this morning, and I longed to hear his voice. We had agreed that we both needed to work on things before we could be together. I knew what I was working on, but he had never told me what he needed to work on. I always thought he had it all together—educated, spiritual, loving, nonjudgmental. What could he possibly need to work on?

***

I woke to the sound of a truck coming up the road. Six o'clock.

Bang, bang, bang.

"Hello, Evie Prince? It's Steve."

"Just a second," I responded in a scratchy voice as I jumped out of bed and grabbed whatever was closest to me. Unfortunately, it was my paint splattered smock.

As I stumbled toward the door, I caught a glimpse of myself in the hall mirror. *My hair!* It was a rat's nest. No time to fix it.

I pulled on a ball cap and answered the door.

Steve let out a slight chuckle. "Good morning. Hope it's not too early?"

"No, no, slept in," I grumbled, trying to make him think I was always up at this time. Then, slipping into a pair of rubber boots by the door, I walked him out to the road. "I assumed you saw the state of the road. Can you help me fill the holes?"

"How do you want them filled? We can scrap the road and level everything out then fill, or we can bring in dirt or rocks."

"I haven't had my coffee yet, but it seems scraping the road would be pretty expensive."

"It can be, but if there is no underground water affecting things, it is the best solution."

"Can you quote me on both and give a timeline?"

"Can do. You said you also need a wooden structure?"

We started walking back up the road. "Yes, I am doing a large painting, and I need something to hold my canvas. My walls are not large enough inside the house, so I need to create a workspace outside."

"Is this all your land?"

"Yup. Why?"

"Why don't you just build a painting studio? It wouldn't have to be too large, but it seems to make more sense, particularly if it rains," he joked. "I built my cousin a big one a few years back. You can see it if you go to her showing next weekend. Just a thought."

"Hmm … I have always wanted a dedicated space for my painting. I don't know if I can afford it just yet, though."

"Can you drive a nail?"

"I can do anything if I put my mind to it," I boasted.

"We might be able to work out a deal. If you have time and are willing to work, I think we can do something."

"Really?" I replied excitedly.

"Wow, I guess that woke you up. Give me a few days, and I will come back with some numbers."

"Steve, I would really appreciate that."

"Anything for Attaquin's family." He looked at his watch. "Oh, geez, I gotta go." With that, he jumped into his truck then rolled down the window. "I'll be in touch in a few days."

"Thank you," I called out as he drove down the road.

I ran back into the house and got dressed. It was still too early to call Hendrix, so I grabbed a couple of muffins then headed over to Granddad's.

Just as I was about to knock, I heard, "Come on in."

"I come bearing presents."

"Whatcha got?"

"I got muffins if you have coffee."

"Done."

We sat at the table, and I shared my morning news.

"That's great. Steve is a good guy," Granddad acknowledged.

"He said something funny."

"What?"

"He said anything for Attaquin's family. What is that about?"

"Oh, it's nothing. I gave him a little help when he first moved to the island. He probably feels like he owes me or something. Sounds to me like he is thinking of an old-fashioned barn raising."

"What is that?"

"It's when you get a group of people together to build a barn. The more people helping, the faster it goes. Since this will be something small, I figured you, me, and Steve can handle it."

"If that's the case, I could probably get Reva to come down and help, as well."

We finished our breakfast, and then Granddad walked me back to the house. We looked around the yard to find the best location for the studio. Then Granddad walked about thirty-five feet from the house.

"Seems like this would give you the most room and the best sunlight. We would have to clear some more of the property, but that shouldn't be a problem."

"Was this land ever cleared?" I probed.

"No, your grandparents liked the seclusion that it provided. Plus, your grandfather didn't like to mow the lawn," he joked.

After Granddad left, it was finally late enough to call Hendrix.

"Good morning," I purred into the phone.

"Good morning, beautiful. I love waking up to your voice. How is your morning so far?"

"I have a lot to tell you." I give him a recap.

"Busy, busy. You said you wanted a studio, and now you are getting one. Nice work."

"Well, I hope to. I still don't know how much—"

"Evie, you have just created this opportunity, don't throw negative energy at it. Believe it will happen, and it will."

"Yes, you are right. Old habits die hard. Hey, can I ask you something?"

"Of course. What's up?"

"Yesterday, when I was sitting at the beach, listening to the sound of the ocean, I thought of you. Since we agreed to work on ourselves before we could be together, I never asked what you are focusing on."

"I am glad you asked. Simply, it is self-worth. Am I worthy of having all this love and joy in my life? The wounds from my childhood run deep. With every beating, I was told I was worthless, that I would never amount to anything, that it would be better if I were dead. Years and years of focus, meditation, study, therapy, and listening to my heart have gotten me this far but, admittedly, when something new and wonderful comes into my life, I fall into old thinking. *You* are that wonderful in my life. I need to believe. No, I need to know that I am deserving of your love. Without that, I cannot give all of me and accept all of you"

My heart raced, thinking of his love. Thinking of our lives together.

I hesitated then asked, "Is that something you will ever overcome?"

"I don't know. Maybe one day. But I want to work through some more things before I totally commit to you."

My silence was deafening.

"Evie, you still there?"

"Yes, I'm here."

"Are you okay?"

"I don't know. I understand what you are saying, because I need to work on that, as well. But you have been working on this for so much longer than me, and you are still not there. I fear we will never be together."

"We will, and it will be sooner than you think. The fact that we are talking about this now means that we are closer than we were before. Love is a powerful thing, and it is the most powerful when it is felt inside. When you love yourself completely. No conditions and no limitations. When that happens, you can give love freely and be okay, even if it is not returned. When you love yourself, you do not look to someone else to give it to you to make you whole. You are already complete. I have learned to love myself more than I did when I was younger, but I still have some work to do."

"I guess we both do," I whispered.

"Don't be sad, beautiful. May I have a hug?"

"Sure." I tried, but my energy just wasn't as high as usual, and I know Hendrix felt it.

"Have a great day, beautiful. I love you, Evie Prince."

There was a silence.

"No need to respond. I know you love me, too," he teased with a cheeky tone in his voice.

"I … I will talk with you later. Have a good day."

After we hung up, I felt confusion and frustration. So, Hendrix wanted to love himself so much that he didn't need my love to make him whole and it didn't matter if I loved him back. Was that how love was supposed to work?

***

To clear my head, I walked back outside to look at the studio location again, noting how much brush would need to be cleared. In the middle of the area was a huge rock. A beautiful grey and mossy rock. I climbed up and perched myself on top of it.

As I tried to steady myself, I realized I had a soundtrack running in the back of my head. *If I don't make him whole, what is to stop him from leaving me? How can I trust he loves me if he loves himself more?* I shook my head to stop the noise, but it continued to get louder. Obviously, being outside wasn't helping me.

I jumped off the rock, but my foot slipped, making me fall face-first onto the ground. "Ouch! Damn, that hurt." I rolled over and noticed dark red blood trickling down my leg. Nothing seemed to be broken, but the gash was pretty ugly.

I limped back to the house to clean and bandage my wound.

The day didn't get better. I burned my lunch and ripped my favorite pair of shorts.

"*Ugh*! What is going on?" I yelled.

"*Negative attracts negative*," I heard in my head. "*Ego doesn't play fair.*"

"I'm not negative," I fumed. "I'm mad."

"*Why are you mad?*"

"Because I love Hendrix, but he doesn't want to need my love."

"*Are you sure you love Hendrix, or do you love the way he makes you feel about yourself?*"

"What is that supposed to mean?"

"*When you can answer that question, you will know.*"

I slammed my hand down on the table.

"Whoa, what is going on in here, kid?"

I looked up to see Granddad looking at me through the screen door. My face was bright red, and my jaw hurt from clenching my teeth.

"Do you want me to go?"

After a few deep breaths, I asked him to come in.

"I came over to see if you wanted to get some ice cream at the cliffs."

I collapsed into the kitchen chair and slumped over, putting my head in my hands. "I don't know what I want."

"Can I help?"

"I don't know. I don't seem to know anything."

"Kid, what happened? You were so happy this morning."

I lifted my head to see pure concern on Granddad's face. "I'm okay. I just don't understand."

"Understand what?"

"Hendrix said something to me today that just got me so upset."

"Okay, do you want to tell me?"

I shared the conversation that Hendrix and I had and how confusing it was to me. Then I explained I had an argument with my higher self.

"And the bandage on your leg?"

"I fell off a rock over where the studio will be."

"So, can you answer the question?" Granddad challenged.

I dropped my head back down into my hands, pulling tightly on my hair. Tears stained my face. "I don't know."

"You don't know, or are you afraid to know?"

A few minutes passed. I wiped my eyes and admitted, "I'm too scared to know."

"Come on; let it all out. What are you feeling?"

"I haven't allowed myself to love anyone for most of my life. Now, when I finally open up and find a man who loves me for me, I am questioned if I really love him. Yes, I love how he makes me feel about myself. Is that wrong?"

"There are no rights and wrongs here. The real question is: do you *need* Hendrix to make you feel this way, or can you feel the same way on your own? Your higher self is pushing you to remember how to love yourself. To not need the love from someone else to make you whole."

"I don't know. He makes me feel like I have never felt before," I admitted.

"I have finally learned, in my many years of life, that love is love pure and simple. When ego enters, it clouds love and puts conditions or limitations on it. People believe that, when they fall in love, it is the other person's love that completes them or makes them happy. True love is when you love yourself completely *and* you *choose* to share your love with someone else. You don't need their love to make you happy. If they were to walk away tomorrow, you would miss them, but you would still have love—the love of self. That is what your higher self is asking you. Do you need Hendrix's love to make you feel complete, or do you complete yourself? You can love Hendrix, but when you love yourself first, the love that you share with him will be even greater." Granddad reached for my hand and gave it a squeeze.

I looked up and gave him a faint smile.

"Come on; grab your ball cap. This old man needs some chocolate ice cream."

CHAPTER 3 — NICE ROAD

"If you don't call me, I am sending the police over," I texted Reva with a big smiley face. Our conversations had been less frequent since things with Brian, the architect divorcee who she had met here on the island, had heated up.

She responded, saying she would call later with the laughing emoji.

Reva was my rock, and I was happy for her. She was always happy with other people's accomplishments and blessings. It was time for her to enjoy some happiness, too.

Today was shopping and fix the car day. I made it down island, shopped, and then stopped by Bread & Spice to grab a few croissants before heading back up island. Before I left the bakery, I asked the cashier if Celeste was working.

"Celeste? No, I'm sorry, she doesn't work here anymore," he quickly replied.

"Oh, is she still on the island?"

"Sorry, I don't know."

"Okay, thanks."

Whoa, that was weird. It was only a few days ago that I had seen her at the cliffs. I hoped she was okay.

The drive up island was stop and go, making me arrive just in time for my car appointment. It was no Meineke, but they got the job done well.

When I finally pulled into the driveway, I saw Steve's truck. He was just sitting there, listening to music.

"Hey."

"Oh, hey. I didn't have your number, so I took a chance and stopped by."

"I hope you weren't waiting long."

"Nope, I was just sitting here, eating my lunch." He held up a half-eaten sandwich. "So, I have some numbers for you regarding the studio."

"Okay, do you mind if we talk in the house? I have to get these groceries inside."

"Oh, sure. Let me help you with those bags."

"Thanks."

Steve followed me in, placing the bags on the counter. "So, as I was saying, I have some numbers for you. Theoretically, we are building a shed, so you will not need to get a permit." He reached into his pocket and pulled out a piece of paper. "Here is the design. It's a smaller version of what I built for my cousin."

"Oh my gosh, this looks beautiful."

"Since you have a south-facing wall, we could put a bunch of windows there and have an open ceiling concept. You can decide later if you want to sheet rock the walls or do anything else. This will give you a structure you can paint in, away from the elements. I would consider this a three-season studio. Winter will be too cold without insulation and a heater."

"Steve, this is amazing. Thank you. How long will it take to build?"

"Once you clear the land, I think we could build it in a couple of weekends."

"I was going to ask my friend to come down to help."

"The more help, the quicker it will get built."

"Steve …" I hesitated. "Why are you doing this? You are so generous with your time, and I don't even know you."

"Like I said, anything for Attaquin's family."

"May I ask, what is the connection to my granddad?"

"He didn't tell you?"

"No, he just said that he helped you out."

"Helped me out is an understatement. Actually, he saved my life."

"What?"

"I was young, on my own for the first time, and had just moved to the island. I got a job doing carpentry. Summer was great. We were busy all the time, but then came my first winter. Things slowed down to almost a standstill. There was nothing to do. I started doing stupid stuff and got hooked. After I checked myself into rehab, Attaquin agreed to be my sponsor when I got out. There were so many times when he had to come save me. And he always did it without judgment. If he hadn't taken the time to help me, I wouldn't be here now."

A warm feeling radiated throughout my body, leaving an enormous smile on my face. "That doesn't surprise me one bit," I uttered.

"So, tell me, how is Attaquin your grandfather?"

"My mother and Attaquin's son had a relationship that no one was aware of. Surprise, then came me. Unfortunately, my dad had lots of demons and couldn't be a father to me, so they kept him a secret. My mother always informed him of what I was doing. When she died, I was sixteen, and that was when I moved here to live with my grandparents, Lilly and Peter Prince. Attaquin was always around, but I just thought he was my grandfather's best friend. When Attaquin was in the hospital, it all was revealed."

"Wow, that is a crazy story."

"Tell me about it; it's my life."

"So, you moved here to be closer to Attaquin?"

"No, this may sound weird, but I am on a journey to find my true self. The things that happened when I was young created a shell, something I could hide in. As I am learning, painting is only one component of me. I am still working on peeling back the layers and finding the others."

"I hear ya. Substance abuse just doesn't happen. It's also a way of hiding. Only until you face your demons can you truly be happy."

We looked at each other with a mutual understanding.

"Are we a go?" he finally asked. "Should I order the materials?"

"Yes!"

"Great. I can help you clear the brush this weekend, but I won't be able to start the actual work until next weekend. I figured we should have this complete by mid-September. What I need you to do is to set up an account next time you are down island with the lumber store. Then I will handle the rest."

"I can't believe this is happening. I wanted a studio, and now I am getting one. Life is good."

"Yes, it is. I will see you Saturday, bright and early."

"Awesome. I will make sure the coffee is ready."

***

I bounced up the steps, doing a little dance into the house, acknowledging that I was really doing this—manifesting my desires. In the distance, I heard my phone ringing, but where was it?

I looked in all the usual places—bag, table, bedroom—but I couldn't find it. Finally, I stopped moving and followed the ringing. In the refrigerator, I found my phone sitting amongst the fresh vegetable. Just as I grabbed it, it stopped.

"Darn, I missed Reva."

I called her back.

"Just missed you," I blurted out when she answered.

"How are you?"

"I am great. And you?" I said in a teasing manner.

"I am wonderful."

"I can feel the glow from here. So, do you guys want to come down next weekend for a visit and help me build my studio?"

"Your what?"

"My studio."

"Wow, someone is moving up in the art world. Congratulations. How did this happen?"

"It's a crazy story, but I met this guy who built one for his cousin. He knows my granddad and will do anything for him. So, we are going to do an old-fashion barn raising. He will help me clear the land this weekend, and we will start building next."

"That sounds amazing. I haven't built anything before, but I am always willing to help. Let me check in with Brian to see if he is available."

"So, is this getting serious?" I asked, knowing full well that it was.

"You could say that."

I screeched with joy. "I am so happy for you!"

"Thank you. It has been a long time coming."

"Just give me enough heads-up on the wedding so I can get my date out here from Colorado."

"Ah … So, that is still going strong?"

"Yes, but we are taking our time. Still working on ourselves."

"I hear you."

"Reva, I know that you have been through a lot, yet you somehow always come out with a smile on your face. How do you do it?"

"Evie, I am just happy to be alive. Every day is a gift, and I try to treat it as such."

"Do you love yourself?" I asked.

"Huh, that's a funny question, but yes, I do. Some days more than others, but yes, I really do. I think that is why it took me so long to find the right person. I met way too many people in my life who just wanted to take. And, because I didn't love myself enough, I would just give, thinking it would make me happy or complete. It was only until I stopped, removed those people from my life, and started giving to myself *and loving myself* that I realized I deserved the very best. Only until I realized I am loved was I able to give love completely."

"And, how did you learn to love yourself?"

"I started small, trying to appreciate something about me every day. I would compliment myself on my hair, or how I did something, the food I cooked. Every time I looked in the mirror, I would find something that I loved about myself. My eyes, or the smoothness of my skin. If you do that enough, you believe it. I learned it is okay to fail and make mistakes because, in the end, they are just learning opportunities. It all comes down to your perspective.

"You have a limited time on this earth; why mistreat yourself? Give yourself grace and enjoy the amazing gifts that you have. Appreciating yourself is the key to loving yourself," she added.

"Wow, just wow," I responded, in complete awe.

"Evie, let me ask you this: can you accept a compliment?"

"Sort of."

"Why is it so hard to acknowledge the fact that you can be good at something or look amazing?"

"I don't know … It just doesn't feel right."

"Because …?"

"Because …" I stammered. "Because I don't believe it."

"I *believe* when you can accept a compliment fully, then you are on the road to loving yourself."

"Reva, as always, thank you."

"It's not a thing."

"Let me know if you guys can make it next weekend."

"Will do. Love ya, girl."

"Love ya, Reva."

***

It had been a heck of a day, and I couldn't get into bed soon enough. Before I turned off the light, though, I sent Hendrix a text.

"I'm sorry."

"For what?"

"I couldn't understand what you were trying to say to me, because my ego got in the way. I know you are doing this so that you can love me unconditionally. Thank you."

"I am doing this for the both of us. When I commit, I want to make sure that I am doing it for all the right reasons."

"I know, and I know what I have to do."

"Good. I love you, Evie Prince."

"I know, and I am working on loving myself, as well. Have a good night."

***

Celeste was on my mind all morning, so I walked up to the cliffs to see if she was working. The day was overcast, so I knew things would be quieter than normal.

Walking into the shop, I looked around, not seeing her. Then, on my way out, I heard, "Evie?"

"Hey, Celeste. How are you?"

"I'm good. Nice to see you again."

"I was hoping to see you. I stopped by the bakery yesterday, and they said you no longer worked there."

"Yes, it's true. I quit."

"Oh no. Is everything okay?"

"Yeah, the owner and I had a falling out. We just aren't on the same page, so I thought it best that I leave."

"What will you do?"

"Luckily, I can pick up extra hours here through the end of September. But, after that, your guess is as good as mine."

"Please, let me know if I can help."

"Thanks. So, what have you been up to?"

"Funny you should ask. I am about to build my own studio."

"Really?"

"Yeah. Amazing, isn't it?" I beamed.

"Who is building it for you?"

"Steve. Steve … I just realized I don't know his last name. He is a volunteer firefighter."

"Oh, Steve Rice. He's a great guy."

"Yes, so I am learning. We are doing a barn raising next weekend. I hope to have a few friends come down to help."

"That's so cool. I'll help. I love working with my hands, and I have done carpentry in the past."

"You would? Wow, that would be amazing."

"Yeah, text me when you get more details. I would be happy to come and help."

We exchanged numbers then said our goodbyes.

Walking back, I gave my appreciation for all the abundance that I had been given and complimented myself on making a new friend.

Strolling back up the dirt road to the house, I was hit upside the head with a feeling of pure panic. Where would Reva and Brian sleep? It was time that I purchased a larger bed for my room, and I needed to get over my anxiety about sleeping in my grandparents' room. Ordering a mattress set was the first thing I could do. Moving into my grandparents' room, though, would still take time.

After dinner, I ordered the mattress. I purchased it off island but, luckily, they could deliver it in time.

While surfing the web, Colbie came to mind. *What was the name of her business?* Energy … Energy something. Finally, it came to me. Energy Works. I searched her website, and a grin crossed my face. The site looked great, and she had lots of positive reviews. Of course, because she was that good.

On the site, I noticed she had a coaching service. If I was going to get past this issue with my grandparents, I needed some help.

After I filled out the intake form, I could make an appointment for a fifteen-minute introductory call. If anyone could help me, Colbie could.

***

The birds woke me out of a deep sleep. Seven o'clock came early. *Thank you, birds, for the wake-up call, because I have a lot to do today.*

I made myself a substantial breakfast then stepped out into the yard within the hour. There was a lot of brush to clear, so I wanted to make a dent before Steve came over this weekend.

The brush was thick, and it didn't seem like I was making any headway. Granddad came over for a bit and helped, but I didn't want him doing too much since it was getting hot out. By eleven, I was done.

I sent my morning text to Hendrix, wishing him a great day. He responded with heart emojis. I loved a man who could be silly.

After lunch, I started rearranging my bedroom to make room for the larger bed. It would be tight, but it was a guest room. Not like someone would stay for a long time.

My phone alarm beeped, telling me I had my introductory call with Colbie in fifteen minutes. I stopped what I was doing and went outside to do a brief clearing meditation. When I opened my eyes, I saw a beautiful monarch butterfly glide by and land on the deck railing. We looked at each other for a moment, and then it flew away. Even I knew that was a good sign.

With just a minute to spare, I went inside and grabbed my phone. The phone rang not long after.

"Hello?"

"Evie?"

"Hey, Colbie. How are you?"

"I thought this number looked familiar. Why did you schedule an introductory call?"

"I need your help."

"Fine, but you know I would help you any time."

"Exactly, I know that, but this is your livelihood now. I wanted to make it official."

She hesitated. "Okay … So, let me explain how I work."

Colbie ran through her process and set expectations on outcomes. I gave her an overview of my needs and what I hoped to get out of these sessions.

"So, my desire is to make this house *my* home, turn what used to be their bedroom into mine, and to let go of any hostility I have toward them so I can make this life my own, free of their fears and expectations."

"Well, that may take a few sessions." She laughed.

"Colbie, in all seriousness, I know you can help me. I need someone to keep me focused since I have been putting this on the back burner. I need this elephant, as they say, out of the room."

"Okay, I understand. How soon do you want to start?"

"Now."

"All righty then. Let me check my schedule to see what time my next session is." I could hear her clicking on the computer. "Okay, my next session is not for another two hours, so you have me for at least one of those."

"Perfect, thank you. I know this may sound weird, but can we work on me making their old bedroom mine as the first goal?"

"Evie, this is a holistic process, so I can't guarantee complete success with that issue first, but we can try."

Colbie started the session with some energy work.

"Did you read the chakra book I gave you? I want to make sure that you remember that you have seven of them, and they are the centers of spiritual power within your body."

"Yes, I read most of it, but I didn't understand how to apply it."

"Well, what I would first like to do is check your chakras to see how your energy is flowing." She began at my root chakra then moved up to my sacral, solar plexus, heart, throat, third eye, and finished at my crown chakra.

"You have blockage in your root and your heart chakras."

"Is that bad? What does it mean?" My tone expressed concern.

"It's not bad; it just means that energy is not flowing how it should in that area. So, let's start with the root chakra. When the root chakra becomes blocked, your home life may feel unsettled. You may also have feelings of not being good enough. However, when it's balanced, you will feel more grounded or stable with a sense of ease, allowing you to face your fears.

"When your heart chakra is out of balance, you may find it hard to forgive or feel empathy, and you could feel anxiety. When the heart chakra is open and balanced, it allows you to open yourself up to the love of others and yourself. You will feel more compassion, kindness, and forgiveness.

"I will send you some meditations to help you focus on those two chakras so that you can learn to open them on your own. I would also encourage you to read about those chakras again so that you can identify when your energy is blocked in those areas. Let's talk again in a few more days so I can see how things are progressing. Please go onto my website and schedule at your convenience," she finished.

"Colbie, this has been wonderful. Thank you for the help. As always, you bring me peace and calmness. I am actually looking forward to working through these issues. I am ready to be free of all this."

"Thank you for trusting me to help you, Evie. I'll talk with you in a few days."

Just talking to Colbie made me feel better.

I went to my bookshelf and grabbed the chakra book that she had given me before I had moved out from Colorado. As I read, it made more sense.

My phone pinged, alerting me to the meditations that Colbie had promised. *Ooo*, she had recorded them. I knew what I was doing tonight.

Before dinner, I popped over to Granddad's, making sure that the brush clearing hadn't been too much for him.

"Come on in."

"How do you do that?" I whined.

He laughed but didn't answer. "What's up, kid?"

"Oh, I just wanted to check in to see how you were doing."

"I'm great. I already ate, but there are leftovers if you are hungry."

"Nope, I'm good. I'm just about to make dinner. I also wanted to say thank you for the guidance you provided regarding

Hendrix. After our chat, I realized I needed to change my perspective."

"Perspective is what this life is all about. You can choose how you want to see it."

"Also, I am working with a friend to help me with my energy, so I can finally accept the things my grandparents did that have affected me and move on."

"Hey, that's good news. I see big changes on the horizon."

"Good ones, I hope."

"That is up to you."

We said our goodnights and, on the way back home, I heard Granddad's words again in my head. *"That is up to you."* It hit me like a ton of bricks.

It was true. I was in charge. How many more times did I need to hear that to finally believe it? Hendrix, Colbie, and Granddad had said this to me before. For whatever reason, it really hit home with me this time. What I did and how I lived my life was one hundred percent up to me.

Back in the house, I made myself a big salad. Before I jumped into the shower, I called Hendrix to tell him the news of the day.

"Evie, I am so proud that you are taking these steps. Sometimes you just can't do it by yourself. Working with someone has helped me in the past."

"Colbie is great, and I wouldn't be here if it wasn't for you and her helping me recognize that painting was my passion."

"So, how is the studio coming along? I wish I could be there to help you."

"I know you do, but I also know you are crazy busy with work. Are you still leading the office in job placements?

"Yes, and the entire office is doing great. Now, that things are opening up, more people are looking for a change. Work life balance and being able to work from home are the big drivers."

"That makes a lot of sense. People are realizing what is truly important in life."

Hendrix paused. "So, is it just you, Steve and your granddad who will build the studio?"

"Actually, Reva, Brian, Granddad, and Celeste all said that they would help."

"Who is Celeste?"

"She is the woman who I went to high school with and works in the shop where I bought your T-shirt."

"Great. Sounds like an amazing group of friends."

"Funny, it really feels like I have made more friends here in six months than I did in six years back in Colorado."

"You are opening yourself up to these people. Don't forget how closed off you were back here in Denver. You were driven by work, and people could see your walls. Those walls are coming down now, and you realized that you actually like people," he teased.

"Ha-ha. Hilarious. I liked people. Just not a lot of them," I admitted.

"Well, I need to leave you. Colbie sent me meditations, and I am excited about getting started. Before I go, may I have a hug?"

"Coming at ya."

Hmm … He gets me every time.

"Have a good night."

"Same to you, beautiful."

After a warm shower, I set myself up on the deck and started listening to the root chakra opening meditation. Her voice was so soothing. Fifteen minutes of pure peace, and I already felt grounded.

Out in the yard, I slipped off my flip flops and let my feet feel the earth. I stood straight, feeling solid and ready for whatever came at me.

***

Another day of slowly clearing brush, and another day of speaking with Colbie.

"So, what did you think of the meditations?"

"I loved them. I felt immediately grounded after listening."

"What you are working through will affect your energy flow, so continue to listen to them. They will help you keep everything open.

"Now, let's chat about sleeping in your grandparents' room. What do you think is holding you back?"

"They were both so private. Growing up, the room was off limits. Now, as an adult and learning about my family and what they did to protect me, I feel even more disconnected from them. Simply, I don't feel welcomed in there."

"So, you say that they did things to protect you. Like what?"

"They didn't tell me about how my mother died or the type of work she was doing when she died, hoping I wouldn't do the same thing. Or that my grandfather did the same humanitarian work. They didn't tell me about my father so that I wouldn't know he was struggling with demons and died from substance abuse. My grandfather told me to give up painting—the gift my grandmother gave me—and get a real job. These secrets made me doubt myself and created a person who was always trying to please my grandfather yet denying my happiness."

"Evie, can you appreciate why they did these things?"

"Yes, as an adult, I can see that they were trying to protect me. But, as a sixteen-year-old when my mother died, and I received no explanation, that really messed with my head."

"You removed all of their personal items from the room, correct?"

"All but my grandmother's jewelry and some of her paintings."

"Will you keep those items?"

"Yes, I would like to."

"What I would like you to do is start moving your personal items into the room. Not all at once, but one item at a time. Bless the item with pure light, healing energy, and love, and put it in a prominent place in the room. Then sit in the room and appreciate the item—how it looks, what you enjoy about it. Each time you put a new item in the room, stay a little longer. Eventually, you will not see the room as your grandparents' but your own. Lastly, in your daily meditations, ask for clarity, empathy, and forgiveness when you think of your grandparents."

"Okay." I let out a sigh of relief. "I can do that."

"Evie, just know that emotions will come when you least expect it. Allow them and feel them, then decide what you will do with them. And, please remember to protect yourself. Now that your chakras are open, you want to protect them.

"This has been a lot today. Be good to yourself. These beliefs that you have about your grandparents were many years in the making. Don't think they will disappear overnight."

"I understand. Thank you!"

***

Steve will not wake me up this time, I said to myself as I made coffee. I saw Granddad slipping through the bushes and, just before he knocked, I called out, "Ready for some coffee?"

He chuckled and smiled. "Ready for today?"

"Yes, I am. Even before I left Colorado, I said I wanted a studio. And now we are here, clearing the land for one."

At six-thirty sharp, I heard something coming up the driveway. Granddad and I went out to see what it was.

"OMG, it's so cute!" I yelled out to Steve as he drove up in a mini backhoe.

He stopped the machine and jumped out. "Good morning, Evie, Attaquin."

"Good morning. Coffee is ready, if you would like some," I told him.

"Yes, please."

"Granddad, do you need a refill?"

"Nope, I am a one cup kinda guy."

I headed inside to grab Steve his coffee and my phone so I could take pictures. When I came out, Granddad was explaining to Steve where we thought the best location would be.

"Sounds like a plan," Steve replied.

"One thing you should know is there is a rather big rock or boulder over there. I don't know if it will need to be moved or not."

"Okay, let me look." He walked over to assess the situation. "Nope, I don't believe we will need to move it."

"Great."

After Steve finished his coffee, he jumped into the backhoe to start work. In no time, the area was cleared. Luckily, the land was reasonably level, so he didn't have to move much dirt.

"Well, that looked easy," I commented.

"When you have someone who knows what they are doing, anything looks easy," Granddad quipped.

"Thanks. Now, let's tackle that road," Steve announced.

"What? The road? But you didn't give me a quote."

"Don't worry; it's covered."

"What do you mean, *it's covered*?"

"You have a benefactor who wanted to help you out."

"Who?"

"Can't tell."

"What? Come on."

"Sorry."

I looked at Granddad, who seemed equally surprised. "Isn't that weird not knowing who paid for this work? I didn't ask anyone for help."

"I guess you didn't need to. Just be happy that you don't have to pay for it."

In another few hours, the road was scraped and leveled out, removing all bumps and holes. When it was all said and done, I skipped down the road, taking it all in. *Universe, thank you for this wonderful gift*, I said to myself.

That night, when I called Hendrix, I just yammered on, not letting him get a word in edge-wise.

"Whoa, whoa, Evie. Slow down."

"Can you believe it? Someone just paid for Steve to level the dirt road. No more holes or bumps."

"And it wasn't your granddad?"

"No, he looked just as surprised as I did by the news."

"Wow, someone is looking out for you."

"Right?"

I shared my ongoing work with Colbie and how I felt like I was making some headway. Slowly, I was becoming more comfortable going in and out of the room. "I actually sat in there and read a book."

"Nice. Are you proud of yourself?"

I grinned. "Yes, I am proud of myself."

"Good. You should be. Remember to celebrate every success."

"I will. Good night, Hendrix."

"Good night, beautiful."

***

A few days later, I met the UPS man out in the driveway, and he handed me a long box.

"Hey, nice road."

"Thank you. Just had it done."

"Have a good day."

"You, too."

In the house, I carefully opened the box. Shelby had come through. It was perfect.

I looked at the calendar on the refrigerator. A little over a month to get this painting done. That shouldn't be a problem … I hoped.

CHAPTER 4 — QUEEN SIZED BED

My work with Colbie was going really well. As she noted, I had mini outbursts of emotions, but I let them come and pass. My decision was not to hold on to those emotions. They resulted from what had happened in the past and I wouldn't let them affect my life from now on.

Between working with Colbie, focusing on keeping my chakras open, and my daily meditation, I felt like I was making genuine progress. Not to mention, I made a point of complimenting myself every day.

I had less than a week before Reva and Brian came to visit, so I needed to focus on being comfortable in that room. Plus, they would deliver the new bed in another day.

I moved the single bed out of my old room then moved my grandparents' bed into that room so my grandparents' room—I mean, my room—would be ready when the new bed arrived.

***

Today had been a long day. They had delivered the lumber, and Steve had given me instructions on how to store it just in case it rained. The new bed had also been delivered, so by nine o'clock, my body was ready for sleep.

Each time I was about to go into the room, I delayed it with more and more things that I needed to do before I went to bed. Subconsciously, I knew what I was doing—nervous about sleeping in there—my new room—when I promised myself that I would do it.

To be more comfortable, I put my favorite sheets on the bed. Crisp white eighteen hundred count Egyptian cotton. To wind down, I then took a leisurely shower and thought about Hendrix. How I longed to be with him again. Maybe I should go back to Colorado after I finished this painting to make sure that our time together here on the island was really real.

I pulled back the covers and slipped into bed. It was firm but comfortable. The night was still warm, and the crisp cold sheets felt good on my skin. However, unable to find a comfortable position, I tossed and turned then stared at the ceiling. The moths banging into the outside light seemed louder than usual. Everything sounded so loud.

What little comfort I had received from the shower dissipated. I sat up and turned on a light. Then I took a few deep breaths and thanked my higher self for giving me the grace and acceptance to overcome this fear.

"Thank you for giving me my space. In time, I know I will open up to you more. But, for now, I need to get used to knowing that this is my home now," I said out loud.

Remembering Colbie's recommendation to protect myself, I visualized stepping into a bright white light, completely surrounded by this light that reached out into the distance in all directions. *Only love can reach me through this light, and only love leaves me through this light.* I was comforted in the thought of this protection, and then I declared, "I am protected."

Making that declaration and giving appreciation allowed me to drift off to sleep.

Lately, I hadn't been remembering my dreams, but tonight, I dreamt in HD. It was like I was watching a movie.

My grandmother was out on the back deck, painting. She slowly turned and looked right at me with her beautiful smile. Then she said, "Evie, always paint from your heart. You see more, and it fills your work with emotion, allowing others to feel what you feel. Do not worry about what others think. I painted with that fear for far too long. Remember, your paintings reflect you in all your beauty and ugliness. Just like in life, not everyone will like you, nor will everyone like your paintings. But there will always be someone who does. And they will be the ones who receive the most from your work. Feel your emotion, and they will, too."

Rolling over, I slowly opened my eyes. Where was I?

Disoriented, my surroundings didn't look familiar. That feeling quickly shifted from confusion to amazement.

She came to me. I felt her presence. I heard her voice. She was with me.

I sat on the side of the bed. "She really came to me," I whispered.

"Thank you, Grandma."

Emotion filled me, and I quietly sobbed, realizing how much I missed her.

"I wish you could be here with me. I need you so much."

In an incredibly soft voice, I heard, "*I am always with you. I am the breeze that moves your hair, the firefly that lights the night. I am everywhere, in everything, and I am always here for you.*"

I texted Colbie with the good news.

"That is wonderful. Keep asking for clarity, love, and forgiveness. I will speak with you next week."

Hendrix was just as happy with my progress.

"Beautiful. Remember to look at any situation through the eyes of love. Things will look different. I am so proud of you. Celebrate every win. Does that mean no more sleeping under the stars?"

***

The big day finally came. Steve said that he could start work a day early.

Granddad, Celeste, Steve, and I stood in front of the lumber pile, tools strewn over the ground. Steve brought his table saw and nail gun, too. We looked like we were ready for building.

Granddad and I worked on cutting the lumber, and Celeste and Steve started nailing the frame for the cement foundation. By lunch, we had the cement poured. It would have to set for the rest of the day, and then we would start framing tomorrow. The timing worked well since I needed to pick up Reva and Brian from the seven o'clock boat.

The end of August was still busy on the island, and weekends were the worst. I stood back from the rest of the crowd, relying on the fact that Reva could see me better as she walked off the boat.

The ferry docked just feet from the busiest part of the island. Passengers disembarked right into a hotbed of activity. It was hard to keep track of everything. Then I heard, "Evie!"

At the top of the stairs were Reva and Brian, waving frantically.

It took them a few minutes to disembark, but when she finally made it over to me, she almost knocked me over. Her hug was huge.

Brian lingered in the background until I told him, "Get over here and give me a hug."

He did so.

"So glad you guys could come down. How was the flight, etcetera.?"

"All good," Brian responded.

Reva was all smiles. Her happiness was infectious.

"Since we're already down here, let's grab dinner before we head up island."

We walked over to the local brewery. The line wasn't too long, and so we were at our table with drinks in less than thirty minutes.

Brian hadn't gotten to see up island on his visit when he had met Reva, so the ride was more of an experience for him.

Reva and I caught up on her work and, in no time, we were driving up the dirt road to my house.

"Hey, what happened to the road?" Reva asked.

"Isn't it wonderful? Smooth as silk."

"How did that happen?"

"I'll explain when we get into the house."

We parked the car, and Brian brought their bags in. I ushered Brian into my *old* room, with Reva following behind.

"Nice, you got a bigger bed. I didn't want to ask before we came. So, where are you sleeping?" Her voice filled with trepidation.

"In my room, of course," I responded off-handedly.

"Very nice. I am so proud of you."

"I am, too!"

Brian just watched us, knowing that he could never keep up.

Reva jumped into the shower before bed. Brian and I sat outside on the deck. This was a perfect opportunity for me to better understand his intentions with Reva.

"Brian, thank you for coming down to help build my painting studio. I really appreciate the help."

"Of course. Reva is always talking about you, so I knew how important it was to support you."

"I don't mean to pry, but I will. Reva is my girl. Actually, she is more than that. She is family. So, what are your intentions?"

Brian gave me an appreciative smile. "My intentions are to make her my wife, if she will have me."

"Okay, that's good to know. But, please know that, if you hurt her, I will personally come after you."

Brian laughed slightly, but then he realized I wasn't kidding.

On cue, Reva joined us on the deck. "What are you all talking about?"

"Not much. Brian and I were just getting to know each other better. We better call it a night. Steve, the guy who is helping me build the studio, will be here by six thirty."

"*Ugh*, six thirty?" Reva whined.

"Yup. Don't worry; coffee and breakfast will be waiting."

***

The full crew was here—Granddad, Steve, Celeste, Reva, and Brian. The floor had been set and today we would raise the walls.

We broke out into two groups. Those who had used a hammer and those who had not. Reva and I served as gofers and official photographers. Steve and Granddad cut the wood, while Celeste and Brian nailed the frames together. With the frames built, we all pitched in to secure them into position.

I stood in the middle of the floor with a grin as big as the Cheshire cat. This was coming together so quickly that it felt unreal.

By the end of the day, we had the four walls up and started securing the rafters for the roof. Tomorrow, we would finish the roof and plywood everything.

"Great work, everyone. Thank you so much for all of your help," I gushed as everyone started packing up.

"Evie, you have a wonderful group of friends. We got further than I had expected," Steve added. "See you all tomorrow. Same bat time, same bat station."

"Unfortunately, I won't be able to join you tomorrow, as I have to work at the shop," Celeste chimed in. "Evie, call me and let me know if you need help during the week."

"No worries, and thank you for all the help today."

Just as Celeste got into her car, I ran over and gave her a big hug. "You didn't have to help on your day off. I really appreciate you."

"Evie, even back in high school, I knew, if given the chance, we could be great friends. It only took twenty-plus years." Celeste laughed.

Once Steve and Celeste had left, Granddad offered to cook everyone dinner.

"It won't be fancy, but I caught a couple of fish yesterday that are just itching to be put on the grill, and I have some quahog chowder."

Before I could say anything, Reva jumped in, "That sounds wonderful. Thank you."

"Granddad, blue plate?" I asked.

"Yup."

"Okay, we will bring the salad and whatever else I can find."

While Reva and Brian showered, I made a quick batch of cornbread, boiled some potatoes, and fried up some salt pork. Nothing better than boiled potatoes with salt pork and drippings drizzled on top. Once they were done, I quickly showered, and then we headed over to Granddad's. Plates in hand, we slipped through the bushes.

Even before I grabbed the door, Granddad said, "Come on in. I was just about to put the fish on the grill."

Brian stayed outside with Granddad to watch the grill master at work, while Reva and I grabbed some beers and set the table.

"So, what were you and Brian really talking about last night?"

"Nothing important. I just told him you were my family, and if he hurt you, I would come after him."

"You did what? No, seriously."

"Yes, seriously. Reva, you only deserve the best, and I will do whatever it takes to make sure that you get that, even if I have to go gangster on him."

"Well, thank you … I guess."

Dinner was amazing, as usual. Granddad was a master at the grill. Brian and Reva couldn't stop raving.

"Mr. Brown, five-star restaurants can't hold a candle to your fish. Thank you."

"Please, call me Attaquin, and all I did was add a little fire. The fish did all the work," he replied with a smile.

We cut the evening short, knowing that six thirty would come really early.

Before the door shut, Granddad yelled out, "See you tomorrow."

I told them to keep going while I popped my head back into the house.

"Granddad, you don't have to help tomorrow. I know today was a lot."

"Please, I am not that old yet. I will see you tomorrow."

I opened the door all the way and gave him a hug.

***

Day two of the build was hairier than the first. Brian and Steve secured the rafters, and I almost couldn't watch. Once done, we covered it all in plywood. Roofing shingles, windows, electricity, and cedar shingles would need to wait until the next weekend. They would install the electricity and windows this week. The last thing of the day was to hang the door.

She was a beautiful little studio. Just perfect for what I needed.

I asked everyone to stand out front, and we took a picture of the crew. Then we called it an early day because Steve needed to get to his cousin's showing. We all agreed to join him a little later.

After Steve left, I suggested we go take a quick swim. Granddad opted out, saying something about rather being on the water than in it.

We didn't even change. Once at the beach, we took off our shoes and jumped right in. The water felt amazing—cold, salty, and wet.

Reva and Brian were swimmers, so they went out farther than I was comfortable with. I sloshed out of the water and did my best to dry off.

Watching the two of them was wonderful. Reva was so happy. *He is good for her*, I thought to myself.

***

We slowed down then pulled off as far as we could on the side of the road. There were over twenty cars lined up. Walking up the road, we saw Steve's truck.

The studio was beautiful, with sky lights and lofted ceilings. Her work was lighted just perfectly on each wall. The music played, and a server brought out drinks and hors d'oeuvres.

Steve saw us and came right over.

"Evie, let me introduce you to my cousin, Beth." He led me through the crowd to a woman standing off to the side.

"Hey, Beth. This is Attaquin's granddaughter. Evie, this is my cousin, Beth."

"Hi, Beth. Your studio is amazing, and your paintings are stunning."

"Evie, so happy you could make it. Steve has been telling me all about your studio. Congratulations. You got one of the best carpenters around to help you," she said with a smile.

"I couldn't agree with you more," I replied.

Steve jumps in, "Okay, enough of that talk. Who wants a drink?"

I looked around, trying to find Reva and Brian. When I didn't see them, I looked out the studio doors to see if they were outside. The sun was setting, and it filled the sky with oranges and reds.

Just as I spotted them, Brian got on one knee.

Without thinking, I announced to the gathering, "He is proposing!"

Everyone ran to the windows to see the special moment.

At that moment, Reva and Brian embraced, and I knew it was a done deal.

I ran outside and grabbed them both in an enormous hug. They both laughed.

I looked at Reva. "I love you, girl, and I am so happy for you!"

I looked at Brian. "Nice job, and welcome to the family."

When we re-entered the studio, the room erupted in applause and whistles, everyone saying *congratulations* to the happy couple. It overwhelmed them. They looked a little embarrassed.

What a special night. I couldn't wait to tell Hendrix about all that had happened.

I left the happy couple to their own devices for the rest of the evening and went up to the lighthouse to meditate and speak with Hendrix.

"Good evening, beautiful. How was your day?"

"Amazing. Such great energy."

"Wow, sorry I missed it. What happened?"

"First, we completed the roof and put up the plywood, had an early evening swim, and then went to Steve's cousin's art show. Last, and most importantly, Reva and Brian got engaged! Right at sunset! It was beautiful."

"That really is an amazing day."

"Right? So, how was your day?"

There was a long silence.

"Hendrix, are you still there?"

"Yup, I am here. Sorry, a text just popped up on my phone from someone from a long time ago." He trailed off.

"Is everything okay?"

"Yeah, yeah. Everything is okay. Hey, Evie, sorry to cut us short, but I have to go. I will call you tomorrow."

"Okay, can I …?" The phone clicked before I could finish my sentence. "Wow."

Trying not to be bothered, I lay on the grass in front of the lighthouse, looking up at the sky, watching. Red, red, white. Red, red, white. As usual, the lights removed any thoughts from my head and lulled me into her light trance.

When I returned, the house was quiet. I slipped into bed, longing for a restful sleep.

***

"Hey, sleepy heads. Time to get up, or you're going to miss your boat!" I yelled.

I could hear stirring, and then Reva shouted, "Shit, Brian, we have to get up."

They both stumbled out of the room, hair crazy, half-dressed.

"Why didn't you wake us up sooner?" Reva complained. "We wanted to have breakfast with you before we left."

"I figured you both needed your sleep. We still have time to grab something at Bread & Spice before you get on the boat."

They finished dressing then threw their stuff in the back of the car. The drive back down island was quiet but peaceful. We parked nearby and walked to Bread & Spice, where we grabbed three ham and cheese croissants and three small coffees. We then sat on the wall and watched the boat slowing come in.

"Thank you so much for making the trip down to help me. When it is all said and done, I will send pictures."

"You better," Reva exclaimed.

"So, when are you going to have your first show?" Brian inquired.

"You need to have lots of paintings before you can show. Currently, I have one. Remember the impetus for building this was so that I could paint my commissioned piece."

"I am sure, by next summer, we will be attending your art show," Brian remarked.

We strolled to the boat and, before they boarded, I gave Reva a big hug. "You did good, girl. Enjoy this ride! I love you."

"I love you, too, Evie. I am so proud of you."

When Brian and I embraced, I whispered in his ear, "Don't make me have to go gangster on you."

"Don't worry; I have been waiting a long time for a love like this."

I watched them board the boat, walking hand in hand. They turned and waved before they went inside.

My heart dropped a little knowing that our relationship would change, but Brian was a good guy. I guessed I could share her with him.

After I got home, I sat outside reflecting on the weekend. Thinking of Reva and Brian gave me inspiration to paint them an engagement gift. Even though I would love to set up in my new studio, I didn't have windows, so it was dark. Besides, the deck was still an amazing place to paint.

I closed my eyes and felt the emotion of seeing the love between the two of them. Reds, oranges, yellow, and a bit of purple were the color pallet for this painting. Their silhouettes, Brian on bended knee. The sunset filled the sky. Energy and love surrounded them.

CHAPTER 5 — TAKE YOUR MEDICINE

Throughout the week, Steve stopped by to install windows, add trim, and to hang cedar shingles. The electrician also stopped by to wire the studio. Now all I needed was the roof to be shingled. The crew would arrive on Saturday. If all went well, we would complete the studio by next Sunday.

I helped Steve install the windows, and I painted the trim. She was a traditional cedar shake building, but I had to add some color. I painted the door a beautiful honey dew melon orange. Just looking at it made me smile.

Saturday came and went as quickly as the roofers installed the roof. It looked like a bona fide studio. Granddad helped me with the landscaping. I installed a stone walkway and mulched the front. Over time, the grass would grow in. Lastly, I planted two hydrangea bushes with the expectation of them either turning purple, blue, or pink.

The night after it was finally complete, I invited Steve, Celeste, and Granddad over for dinner. We celebrated and took pictures. She was beautiful, and I called her the Sunshine Studio. Celeste took a picture of me in front for my announcement card.

Dinner with my new friends was perfect. We laughed, and Granddad teased me about how I measured once and cut twice versus the industry standard of measuring twice and cutting once. I wished Reva and Brian could have joined us, but they were in the throes of figuring out their new life together.

After we said our goodnights, I texted Hendrix the photo. Since our discussion last week, he had been preoccupied, so our communications had been short and sporadic. He reassured me that everything was okay, so all I could do was believe him.

Before bed, I went over to the studio and sat in the middle of the floor, thanking my higher self for the guidance and support in manifesting this amazing studio. "I create beauty in this room," I declared.

Bright and early, I looked out the window to make sure the studio was still there. A smile crossed my face when I saw the brightly painted door.

After breakfast, I grabbed the canvas and hung it in the studio. It was time to get to work on this piece.

The information that Tatum had sent me had my mind racing. Modern hotel lobby, dark colors, moody. What was I supposed to do with all this? I didn't know where to start.

Time seemed to pass slowly as I stared at the canvas. To give myself a break, I checked my phone. I hadn't realized that Hendrix had texted me. His response to the picture had been a thumbs-up. *A thumbs up? WTF is that about.* Something that I had been dreaming about had just manifested, and he gave me a thumbs-up? I didn't know what the hell was going on with him, but I was about to find out.

I dialed his number. It rang many times then flipped to voicemail.

"Hendrix, it's Evie. There is obviously something going on there. I am worried, and I hope you are okay. Call me. We need to talk."

Later that afternoon, I received a text from Hendrix.

"Evie, I am okay. Please do not worry. I can't talk now, but I will call you in a couple of days. Don't worry; everything is okay."

After reading his text, I didn't know whether to be concerned or livid. I was leaning toward livid, but I knew, deep down, that there had to be a good reason why he was acting this way.

To clear my head and focus on what I needed to do, I took a walk on the beach, hoping to find some inspiration. The beach was quiet. Summer was just about over. School was starting and all the summer dinks had headed home.

I had hoped the beach would calm me, but I couldn't quiet my mind. All I could think about was Hendrix. Why was he acting so weird? Was he ghosting me? Was it over and he couldn't tell me? Had he found someone new? All these questions, but no answers.

My anxiety grew, and I felt faint. My heart thumped in my chest. I stopped in my tracks and sat down before I could fall down. I put my head between my knees to steady myself and tried to breathe.

When I looked up, I saw the lighthouse in the distance. Red, red, white. Red, red, white. I got lost in her light, and my mind slowed.

It had been a long time since I had freaked out, and I knew that ego was messing with me. I needed to turn off the head and listen to the heart. This was exactly what my higher self asked me about. *Do I need Hendrix's love to be whole, or do I make myself whole?* Right at that moment, I chose to make myself whole.

***

"Evie, it's so nice to hear from you. How are things going on the Vineyard?"

"Life is fantastic, Tatum. Sorry I have been absent."

"No worries. I hoped you were just in a creative space, so I left you alone. How is the painting coming?"

"It's coming," I mumbled.

"First, let me be a friend. Are you okay?"

"Yes, I'm good. A lot has been going on."

"I can tell. Thanks for sending the picture of the Sunshine Studio. I am so happy that you have created a wonderful space for yourself."

"Thanks. Now that the studio is completed, and I have time to paint, I still don't know what to paint."

"Evie, take your time. You can do this. I have all the faith in the world that you will create something amazing. Now I need to be your agent. Please stay in touch. The buyer would love to have the painting early. I just need to set expectations."

"I understand and will keep you informed from now on."

"I don't want this to sound too glib, but I have learned from some of my other artists that the hardest part is to take the first stroke. Throw some paint on the canvas and see where it takes you."

"Thank you for your understanding and the advice, Tatum. I will definitely try that and see where it leads me."

***

Thursday was my next planned discussion with Colbie, but I needed her guidance now. So, I texted her, asking if I could cash in a friend chit and speak with her without an appointment. She called me right back.

"Evie, what's up? Is everything okay?"

"So much to tell you. Don't really know where to start."

"The beginning works best."

"Okay." I started with the weirdness with Hendrix, my declaration to love myself completely, and the fact that I didn't know what to paint for this commissioned piece. "Colbie, I just feel like there is something holding me back."

"Do you feel it is Hendrix? Is that uncertainty making you feel that way?"

"Not really. His behavior gives me concern, but he has never affected my painting."

"I want you to try something with me, Evie. Close your eyes and take some deep breaths. Put your hand on your heart center, and I want you to say in your mind: Higher self, what is holding me back from painting? Breathe and listen. What do you hear?"

A few moments passed, and then I responded, "I'm afraid the buyer won't like it. My grandfather's criticism rings in my head. I don't want to let anyone down."

"Good. Now we know where to start. When we speak again, that is what we will focus on—your relationship with your grandfather. Continue with your meditations, and I will talk with you in a few days."

"Thanks, Colbie. I appreciate you more than you could ever know."

***

It was time. I needed more answers.

Slipping through the bushes, I headed over to Granddad's. Then, when I got to the door, fully expecting him to say, "Come on in," there was nothing. Maybe he didn't hear me.

I knocked. Then I heard, "Who is it?" coming from the back room.

"Granddad, it's Evie. Can I come in?"

I heard some rustling, and then I saw him come out of his bedroom.

"I'm sorry, Granddad. Were you asleep?"

"No, just resting."

"But it's the middle of the day. Are you feeling okay?" I asked as I stepped into the house.

"Yup, just a little tired."

"Granddad, did you take your medicine?" I questioned.

"I was."

"What do you mean, *was*?"

"I was feeling fantastic, strong, so I stopped taking it when I ran out."

"What? Granddad, you need to take that medicine for the rest of your life. You just can't stop." The volume of my voice increased. "Where is your prescription?"

"In the bathroom."

"Let me call your doctor to see what we need to do. You need to get back in bed," I commanded, grabbing my phone and dialing Dr. Chase's number.

"Hello, my name is Evie Prince. I am Attaquin Brown's granddaughter. My granddad is feeling very weak. He stopped taking his medicine and desperately needs a refill."

The nurse put me on hold for a few minutes then came back, saying we needed to get him to the hospital as soon as possible. They would alert the hospital that he was coming.

"Granddad, we need to get you to the hospital. Let's grab some of your things and head down."

"Evie, please, kid, it's nothing. Let's just fill the prescription and call it a day."

"I don't know who you think you're dealing with. I am not taking no for an answer. If you refuse, then I will just call for the ambulance. It's up to you. Either we go in my car, or you take the ambulance and the entire town knows, including Steve, that you are going to the hospital." I stand there with hands on my hips, the look in my eyes letting Granddad know I was not messing around.

"Okay, kid. Grab my bag in the closet. My pajamas and robe are behind the door."

"Yup, yup. Been through this drill before."

When we arrived at the hospital, Granddad was immediately taken into a room. They hooked him up with monitors and started running test.

Dr. Chase came into the room after he had received the results.

"Attaquin Brown, do you want to explain what this is all about? Did you miss the part in my instructions where I said that you would need to take this medication *for the rest of your life*?" His voice boomed.

"Doc …" Granddad whined.

"Geez, Attaquin. Are you ready to ship out or something?"

"No, not yet. I've got this beautiful granddaughter here to keep an eye on."

Dr. Chase looked over at me and smiled. "Well, it's a good thing your granddaughter is smarter than you. You could have really caused some problems. I am keeping you overnight for monitoring. You have received today's dosage of medicine, and your granddaughter can get the rest of your prescription filled over at the pharmacy. Don't make me have to come all the way up island to make sure you are taking care of yourself."

"Yes, Doctor," Granddad replied like he was a scolded child.

"Granddaughter, please join me outside in the hall."

Granddad gave me a sheepish look.

When I stepped out into the hall, Dr. Chase's expression became serious. "Your name is …?"

"Evie, Evie Prince."

"Evie, it was a good thing you brought your grandfather in when you did. It is no joke about his medication. He needs to be diligent, and if you see signs of weakness again, get him right back here."

"Is his heart murmur getting worse?"

"Well, at his age, they don't get better. We all want Attaquin to be around for a long time, but if he pulls another stunt like this, I'm afraid to say that things will go downhill fast. Keep him quiet for the next week. I want you to schedule an appointment at my office in another couple of weeks to make sure the medication is doing what it needs to do. If at any time he becomes weak, or not his ornery self, bring him back to the hospital."

"Thank you, Doctor. I appreciate all of your help."

"Attaquin is very special to many people. We all want to make sure that we get many more years with him."

Before I went back into Granddad's room, I texted Steve, letting him know what was going on and asked that he stop by in a few days to check in.

When I came back in, Granddad's back was to me.

"How are you feeling?"

"Better. Not as tired."

"Seriously, Granddad, what were you thinking? Why did you stop?"

"I don't like having to take all that medication. I wanted to see if I could do without it," he grumbled.

"Yeah, and …?"

"What do you mean, *and*?"

"I know you are not telling me everything. What is really bothering you?"

He rolled over and looked at me. "I don't want to get old. I finally have you in my life. From the moment that I looked into your eyes when they brought you home from the hospital, I wanted you in my life, but we made our decisions. I want to fix whatever we didn't do right by you, and that is going to take time. Time that I'm afraid I may not have."

I grabbed Granddad's hand and held it tightly. "You were always special to me growing up. You understood me. I knew I could always count on you. It may not have been perfect, and yes, there is still so much I need to understand, but you have given me so much more than you know. I want you around for a long time, as well. To make sure that happens, *take your medicine*!"

"Okay, okay. I should know better than to cross a Prince/Brown woman."

CHAPTER 6 — LET IT GO

The week after Granddad returned home from the hospital, we both took it easy. I cooked and cleaned for him and, on some days, almost had to forcibly make him rest.

"Kid, can't an old man be let out for good behavior? I need to go fishing."

"Sorry, Granddad, not until you see Dr. Chase in another week can you go out on the boat."

"Don't you miss fish? Don't you miss chowder?"

"Yes, I do. How about I buy some quahogs, and then you can teach me how to make your chowder?"

"You want to buy hogs when we can just go and get them ourselves?"

"All right, you teach me how to hog, and then you can make the chowder. Deal?"

"Deal!"

We loaded Granddad's truck with his rake and basket then drove down to the creek. I had put the town pass in the truck so we wouldn't have any issues.

I carried everything down to the beach. It was low tide, so I could walk out far.

When I got into the water, Granddad said, "Feel around with your feet in the sand. You can feel the hogs. Once you find one, use the rake to lift it from the sand."

"Oh, I think I found one." I grabbed the rake and started moving the sand. When I reached into the water, there it was, my first hog. I victoriously held it up so Granddad could see.

"At this rate, we'll have chowder next week," he teased.

"Okay, okay." I took the hint and got serious.

In under an hour, I collected enough hogs for a nice pot of chowder. My job done, now it was up to Granddad to shuck and make the chowder.

"So, are you going to show me how it's done? Or is it still a secret?" I asked tentatively.

"The biggest secret to my chowder is getting the hogs yourself. I don't do anything special. Simple. No gourmet frou frou stuff. Grab yourself a beer and watch."

I did as I was told and watched Granddad in his element. In no time, he had shucked the hogs and was chopping them for the chowder. The simplicity of the chowder was incredible. It truly came down to the freshness of the hogs. Grandma would be so jealous that I had finally gotten the recipe.

I left Granddad to raid my refrigerator then made biscuits and a salad. Before I even got into his house, I could smell the aroma from the chowder. Mmm …

We enjoyed dinner and each other's company.

"Granddad, I want to learn more about my grandmother and grandfather."

"What do you want to know?" he asked.

"When I was going through the chest, I saw their wedding pictures and early life. I also found my grandfather's postcard from South America to my grandmother. Did you know him then?"

"I met your grandfather in Vietnam. We served together and basically became brothers. I told your father about the island and, when he got out, he and Lilly moved here."

"Why was he so against my mother doing humanitarian work when he had done the same thing? Was it because she was a woman?"

"No, no. He saw horrible things in South America and Vietnam and hated having to go to war. He saw firsthand what it did to people on both sides and didn't want your mother to see or be hurt by it. Then, unfortunately, his worst nightmare came true. That's why it was decided at the start that you would not know of your mother's work."

Granddad looked off into the distance. "Evie, what you don't know is, at a very early age, you had the same free spirit that your mother had. Your grandfather, Peter, saw it and was scared of it. He wanted to make sure you were safe."

"Just because I *was* a free spirit, did not mean that I would do as my mother."

"True, but your grandfather couldn't take that chance. I remember he and your grandmother arguing over whether she should teach you how to paint. That creativity and hunger to see was in you, and he felt that, if you painted, it would lead to other things. When your grandmother passed, it was his opportunity to make sure that he steered you in another direction, one that would keep you safe."

Shock took over me. I sat in silence. Then I felt pure anger.

"He basically ruined my life!"

"That's not how he saw it. He felt he saved your life."

I didn't know what to do or say.

Granddad continued, "Evie, you can't imagine the horror that your grandfather experienced. He would do anything, even endure the anger and hate from his own grandchild, before he would let something bad happen to you."

As an adult, I could understand what Granddad was saying, but my childhood feelings came back—confined, hurt, lonely, and confused.

"Granddad, I also found a pocketknife that was inscribed."

Before I could continue, he said, "*Share your light.*"

"Yes, what was that about?"

"Your grandmother, Lilly, gave that to him before he left. Your grandfather was as much of a free spirit as your mother and you. Lilly supported him and knew that he needed to do that work to be his true self.

"Evie, your grandfather's fears were not unwarranted. He did it, your mother did it, so there was a good chance that you would want to do it, as well."

That was all I could handle for one night.

Granddad and I did the dishes in silence.

I was halfway out the door when he said, "Your grandfather was not an evil man. He was scared. Scared to lose the thing he loved more than himself. Please try to remember that."

All I could hear was Hendrix saying, "*Look at everything through the lens of love. It will look different.*"

Normally, I would have had a long conversation with Hendrix about this news, but I kept it to myself. He was going through whatever he needed to, and I needed to do the same.

Before I went to sleep, I grabbed a glass of water. On the windowsill was my grandfather's knife. I examined it and tried to feel the energy from it. Then I put it on my bedside table and crawled into bed.

With a deep breath, I looked at this new information with love. Before I fell asleep, I protected myself then asked my higher self for clarity and guidance. Sleep came quickly.

Flashes of light, screams, children running. Images popped in and out of my head. Confusion, fear, death. I woke to the sound of my voice, tears streaming down my face. It was still dark.

I flicked the light on and sat up in bed. My heart was pounding, and I felt cold and drained. I drew my knees into my chest and sobbed. My body ached with pain.

***

My discussion with Colbie revealed a lot. She was proud that I had the courage to learn more about my grandfather and that I had looked at the information through the eyes of love.

"You will still have to process this more, but can you understand why he did what he did?"

"Yes, but I have to wonder what my life would have been like if he hadn't taken such extreme measures."

"They seem extreme to you, but to him, he had to make sure. Plus, you will never know what your life would have been like."

"I may have been an artist."

"Yes, but would you have been the same artist you are today? When you painted in college, you said you sold nothing. But now, you have sold every piece you have put up for sale. Don't lose sleep over the what ifs. Live in the present. Experience the now."

"I hear you, and that is what I need to focus on the most."

"What do you think about your dream?"

"It was horrible. I woke so confused, scared, and in pain."

"You don't realize how powerful you are. I believe you were taking the memories or energy from your grandfather's knife. If that were true, does that give you an understanding of the fear that your grandfather had?"

Unable to answer, I could feel the lump growing larger in my throat. The pain from my dream had given me a glimpse of what my grandfather had felt. My tears were uncontrollable.

"For so long, I had such anger against my grandfather. I thought I could never please him. But all he cared about was me being safe, not if I got a promotion or landed the big sale. All he wanted to know was that I was safe," I sobbed out.

"Tonight, before you go to sleep, protect yourself then ask your higher self to bring your grandfather to you. Speaking with him will provide you with what you are looking for."

As guided, I protected myself and asked that my grandfather to visit me in my sleep. Before I drifted off, I heard a familiar voice.

"Evie, my love, I am sorry that I hurt you. You are my heart. I have always been proud of you, but my fear turned my love into pain for you. Please forgive me."

It was not until the morning that I realized he had come to me. However, unlike the joy that I had felt when my grandmother had come, this time, I felt sorrow. I felt sad for my grandfather to live with that fear his entire life. That fear that killed his own daughter and the fear that maybe I would have the same fate.

"Grandfather, I love you," was all I could say.

***

"*I love you, Evie Prince*" came across my phone screen. It had been well over two weeks since I had spoken regularly to Hendrix. His text normally would have made me feel all warm and fuzzy, but not today. My response was heartfelt but distant.

"*I hope you are well.*"

I solicited nothing further from him. If he wanted to engage me, he would have to do more than send a text.

A few moments later, the phone rang, and it was Hendrix.

"Hello."

"Hi, beautiful. How are you?"

"Well. And you?"

"Evie, please don't be mad."

"I am not mad. That happened about two weeks ago. Now I am indifferent." I knew my words hurt him, but I had been through enough emotion, and I didn't want to add more to the pile.

"Evie, I know I owe you an explanation, and I am fully prepared to give you one. There has been a lot of things that I needed to sort out. I didn't want to bring you into the mess."

"But if you loved me, why would you want to hide anything from me?"

"I just wanted to protect you."

"You know what?" I snapped. "I am so sick and tired of people feeling the need to protect me. Am I weak? Will I break? No, it is just *your* own fear. It scared you to tell me. Admit it!"

There was a long silence. Then Hendrix cleared his throat. "Yes, Evie, you're correct. I am scared. Scared of what you will think of me. Scared that I don't deserve your love. I am scared that you will leave me."

His honesty removed the venom from my voice. "I don't know what happened, but I am here for you. I don't promise you anything other than I am here for you."

"I understand, and that is all that I could ask," he replied.

"Start from the beginning," I instructed.

He sighed before beginning, "About a month ago, a woman who I knew before I met you contacted me. We'd had a brief relationship, but neither of us were in a good place to be serious. We stayed in touch and would see each other now and again. I guess you could say friends with benefits. As I continued to turn my life around, I didn't want to have that type of relationship. We tried to be committed, but it didn't work. We agreed to stay friends, and we went to live our own lives. The reason for her contacting me was that, unbeknownst to me, she got pregnant and had a little girl. She believed it was my child."

I didn't say a word. I couldn't say anything. All I could do was breathe.

"Evie, you still there?"

"Continue."

"We did the paternity tests, and it's true. She is my child. She admitted that, if she didn't need me, I would never have found out about the child." He paused before choking out, "My daughter has cancer, and her mother can't afford the treatments."

My head was swirling, and I felt faint. I sat down and put my head on the table.

"How old is she?" I whispered.

"Three years old."

"Her name?"

"Aja."

"That is a pretty name."

"Evie, are you okay?"

"No, I am not, but it is not me you need to worry about. Take care of your daughter. She needs you."

"But you said that you would be here for me."

"I am, but I can't tell you in what capacity yet. Give me time to process all this. I am here but don't expect to hear from me every day. Take care of you and your family. They need you." That said, I ended the call.

***

"How much more emotional shit can I handle?" I yelled at the top of my lungs.

"*You can handle all that is given,*" I heard in my head.

"Really? Really? What have I done to deserve all this sorrow and pain?"

"*Is it any more than you have endured before? You are not the cause of these things. You are experiencing the feelings from these things, but you can change how you feel.*"

"What am I supposed to say? It's not my problem? Life is all rainbows and lollipops and move on?"

"*You are on this earth to experience life to its fullest. What you consider good or bad, whichever it is, it's an experience. Once you have experienced it, you can now choose what you do with it. Continue to feel the pain and make it your own, or take note and allow it to pass through. It is done, and there is nothing you can do to change it. But you can change how you react and move forward.*"

***

I needed to get this out. I needed to paint.

Looking at the blank canvas, all I wanted to do was to destroy the hurt and pain that I felt. Therefore, I threw color after color against the canvas, splattering paint *everywhere*. My strokes followed my emotions—elation, pain, confusion, love.

Stepping back, it looked like a mess. No rhyme or reason. Just conflict.

I opened the door to get fresh air and realized that I had been in the studio for hours.

Inside the house, Granddad had left me a plate. I picked at the food, but I had no appetite. The emotions that were flowing within me were still so raw.

I didn't want to feel this way. I wanted to love. To love Hendrix and my grandparents unconditionally. What had happened was not my fault. I did not have to feel guilt or try to make things better. I needed to love to save myself.

"*I love you, Hendrix Talisman,*" was all I said.

I didn't expect him to respond. That text was for me. To show myself how far I had come.

Hendrix didn't make me whole; *I* made myself whole, and I had chosen to share my love with him, if he loved me or not.

***

"Come on in," Granddad telepathically said.

"How are you feeling today?"

"Good."

"Ready to see Dr. Chase?"

"Sure," he mumbled.

"Granddad, why do you give Dr. Chase so much flack? He really cares about you."

"Uh-huh."

"He said something interesting to me when we were down at the hospital, that you were special to many people. I know there is a story behind that statement. Want to share?"

"Nope."

"Okay …" I trailed off. "Either way, we need to get going. Don't wanna be late for your appointment."

"*Hmph.*"

At the doctor's office, everyone knew Granddad.

A young intern took us into an examining room.

"Mr. Brown, I will join Dr. Chase in your examination today. I have heard so much about you."

"Oh really? What exactly have you heard?"

"That you are a well-known fisherman, a war hero, that you will keep us on our toes, and that you are always willing to help people in need."

"I don't know who said all that. They probably got me confused with someone else."

At that moment, Dr. Chase chimed in, "Oh, he forgot to say that you are also an ornery SOB."

The intern lowered his head so that Granddad couldn't see him smile.

"I need to hang out with these people so that I can learn more about you," I said under my breath.

"So, Attaquin, how are you feeling?"

"As strong as a horse," Granddad boasted.

"Any feelings of weakness or being overly tired?"

"Nope."

"Taking your medicine?"

"Yup."

"Good. We will take you down to run a few tests to make sure all is working as it should. Evie, you can sit in the waiting area while we're gone."

Granddad looked at me like "*Oh yeah, here we go again*," and I tried not to laugh.

The intern accompanied Granddad back to the waiting room. Dr. Chase followed behind.

***

"All looks good," Dr. Chase announced half an hour later.

"Great." I beamed.

"So, Doc, can I finally go fishing?"

"Yes, you are all cleared."

"Finally," Granddad muttered.

Dr. Chase looked over at me. "Keep him honest and make sure he takes his medicine regularly."

"Will do, and thank you both."

On the ride home, Granddad seemed agitated, muttering under his breath.

"What's up? Why are you so grumbly?" I asked.

"That Dr. Chase drives me crazy. Acts like he is a friend or something."

"So, he's not?"

"He is a good doctor, but that's it."

"Seriously, Granddad, what's going on?"

"Fine, I don't like that man."

"Obviously, but why?"

"When you were born, he was the attending physician. Your mother had complications giving birth to you. We had concerns that you may have health issues. I heard him say to the nurses that he wouldn't be surprised. Said the father was indigenous and alluded that my son—your father—was an alcoholic. A drunk Indian. I looked at him, and he knew I heard it. He won't admit it, but down deep, I know he is racist."

"Oh, Granddad. I'm sorry. I would have called another doctor if I had known."

"Kid, we don't have that many. Don't worry about it."

We drove in silence, but I could feel that Granddad was seething at just thinking about it again.

"Hey, remember the day I was bringing you home from the hospital the first time, and when we crossed the town line, you exhaled loudly, saying you didn't want to bring the craziness of down island home with you?"

"Yup."

"Well, I don't want you bringing that home with us. Let it go, for you and me, let it go."

Granddad looked at me and smiled. Then he closed his eyes and exhaled.

CHAPTER 7 — BIG BEAR

The night was beautiful as I sat out on the deck and watched the sunset, memories flooding my mind. My grandfather taking me to get ice cream. Grandmother teaching me a new painting technique. How my grandfather would tease that she was keeping this family afloat by selling her paintings. Then Hendrix crossed my mind.

I missed him. He hadn't responded to my text, but I hadn't expected him to, either. I had the impulse to send him some healing energy.

My energy rose, thinking of the times we spent together. My torso tightened, and I released that energy, sending it to him. Sending him love and healing light. As I opened my eyes, I saw her light. Red, red, white.

That was it. I knew how to bring my painting together!

I walked into the studio and readied my paints. Looking at what I had done, I could feel the anxiety, fear, and confusion. From that emotion, I brought in the healing light of the lighthouse. She had been my rock for as long as I could remember. She calmed me then and continued to do so now. Her silent strength was my protector, and the glow from her lights was her love showing me the way. Her light gave warning and protection to the many who dared to sail the rocky waters. My desire was that her light would do the same to all who saw this painting.

Before I took pictures to send to Tatum, I asked Granddad to come see the painting. I waited outside so that he could feel it alone, with no commentary from me. He seemed like he was in there forever. When he came out, his eyes were red.

"Granddad, everything okay?"

He smirked. "Yeah kid."

"What's wrong?"

"It gives me such joy to see you be the amazing artist we all knew you could be. Your grandmother and I would discuss your talent in secret, away from your grandfather. She knew you were talented and all she could hope for was that you painted your truth. Not what was expected by others, but the emotion you felt." He looked at me tenderly, and my eyes welled up. "Your grandmother felt trapped. She was exceptionally talented, as well, but they lived here, and only a few saw her work. To sell, she painted what they wanted, not what she felt in her heart. She is so proud to know that you are painting from your heart, doing something that she was not strong enough to do herself."

Just then, I realized the paintings that I had found in the back of the closet were what Granddad was talking about. She had been finally painting her truth at the end of her physical life. She had finally allowed herself to be.

Granddad put his arm around my shoulders and led me into the house. "Kid, open the trunk. In there, you will find something wrapped in a brown paper bag."

I did as I was told. Before I could open it, though, Granddad quietly walked out.

I slowly opened the wrapping that carefully protected a small painting. When I saw it, I trembled. I couldn't believe my eyes. It was a painting amazingly similar to what I had just painted. Different colors, but the feeling of confusion, confinement, then freedom and love leapt off the canvas. How could this be?

***

I took a photo of the painting and sent it to Tatum. Admittedly, I felt nervousness that it wasn't what he was looking for, but I painted it for me, so be it.

It took Tatum an hour to respond. I truly waited with bated breath.

"Magnificent!"

"Will he like it?"

"I believe this is better than what he expected. Let me figure out the logistics to get this packaged and shipped. I will forward his response. Congratulations, Evie, you did a spectacular job."

I had expected to take a trip back to Denver once I had completed the painting, but that seemed off the table now.

To support Hendrix and his daughter, I vowed to send them as much healing energy as I could every day. He might not want to hear from me, but he would feel me often.

My phone flashed.

"It's Nik. Can I call you?"

I replied immediately with, *"Yes!"*

"Hey, Evie. How are you?"

"I'm great. But, what about you? I haven't spoken to you since I left Denver."

"I am healthy and happy, thanks for asking. The reason for my call is that my brother is a mess. I know something happened between the two of you. I don't want to pry, but he really needs you. Aja's cancer is really taking a toll on him."

"Nik, thanks for reaching out. Neither one of us may have handled this situation *correctly*, but I promised I would be there for him. I just don't think that he wants to hear from me now. In my pain, I said some hurtful things."

"He gave me a little information, but not everything. What he told me is that he felt your energy, and it helped him. I know what your energy did for me when I was in the hospital, so I am calling to ask that you send him and Aja more of that."

"Funny you should ask. I vowed to do that already. I hoped it helped, but I don't think he would have told me if it did."

"He is hurt, but he is more mad at himself. He wanted to trust that the feelings you had for each other would be enough to get through this situation, but he wasn't sure and got scared."

"I am also hurt and angry. Hurt that he didn't trust us, and angry at myself for shutting him down immediately. But I needed time to process."

"So? Didn't he?"

"I don't think I was strong enough to handle it any other way."

"I'm not here to judge either of you. All I know is that you and Hendrix need to be together. He needs you."

As soon as we hung up, I checked flights to Denver. I didn't know where this would take us, but I had to try it.

***

I arrived at DIA and got a rental car. Colbie had invited me to stay with her and the boys.

I texted Nik that I had arrived safe and sound, and she said she would let me know when Hendrix would be at the hospital.

Seeing Colbie felt safe and warm. She looked great, and the boys were growing into polite young men.

"So, when will you see Hendrix?"

"His sister, Nikki, will call me and let me know when he will be at the hospital."

"Do you think it's good to just surprise him like this?"

"I don't think he will accept my presence any other way. If he asks me to leave, I will obey his wishes. If he is okay for me to stay, then I will do so. I have no expectations either way. It is truly up to him how I support him. Plus, he would never have asked me to come all this way out here. Hopefully, he will appreciate that I am here for him."

We had a wonderful dinner and caught up on the happenings of our old company and how her new business was coming along.

"Did you finish your commissioned piece?"

"Yes, I did. It was a true labor of love. I had to love myself to finish it." I grabbed my phone to show her a picture.

"Evie, this is remarkable. As always, the emotion is palatable. Did the buyer like it?"

"I don't know. I'm still waiting to hear from my agent."

"I'm sure he'll love it. It is striking."

In the middle of our conversation, I received a text from Nikki.

"Hendrix will be at the hospital in the morning, by nine o'clock. I would suggest, after you get there, to text him to meet you in the lobby and see how it goes. Good luck."

By eight o'clock, I was already out the door. Life was getting back to its old pace now that people were working in person, and I didn't want to get caught in traffic.

I loaded a giant bear in the passenger seat that I had purchased from the toy store near the airport. Then, nine o'clock on the dot, I was in the lobby.

I tried to keep myself out of sight, but it was difficult with a giant bear in my lap. As each person walked in, I slunk down. It was a busy morning, so I was ducking and bobbing nonstop. Then I saw him.

He still made my heart jump. Handsome, but I could see how tired and stressed he was.

It didn't matter if I was standing naked in the lobby, he would not have seen me. He was a man on a mission.

Now that I knew he was here, I relaxed and went to the coffee shop to grab two cups of coffee. Then I found a quiet corner back in the lobby and texted him.

"Good morning. Can I buy you a cup of coffee?"

There was no immediate response, so I sat there patiently, breathing and trying to calm myself. I wanted to see him desperately, but I didn't know how he would react. Would he reject me, or would he welcome me? Finally, he responded.

"What?"

"May I buy you a cup of coffee?"

"Evie, I don't have time, nor the patience, for cute banter."

"Understood. I am in the lobby with a cup of coffee for you, and I have a present for Aja. Please let me know if I should leave it at the front desk of the children's ward or if you would like to come down to the lobby."

Ten minutes later, there was still no response. *Well, I guess that didn't go as well as I had hoped,* I said to myself.

Just as I was getting ready to deliver the coffee and bear to the front desk, I saw Hendrix stepping off the elevator. Our eyes locked. Then he came over to me, and both of us just stood there awkwardly. There were no big, warm hugs; just discomfort.

"Wha …? What are you doing here?" he stuttered.

"I told you I would support you. This is the best way that I knew how. You can ask me to leave, and I would understand. Just say the word." I handed him the bear and the coffee.

He just stared at me.

"Okay, I guess no words are needed. Take care of yourself and your little girl," I said as I turned and walked away.

When I got back in my car, I fell apart, tears spilling from my eyes. My chest hurt from crying. I needed to control myself, as I was in no condition to drive.

Once I pulled myself together, I grabbed my phone to text Nik to let her know I was leaving in the morning, finding a text from Hendrix. All it said was, *"Please don't go."*

***

Back at Colbie's, the house was quiet. I meditated and cleared my head.

Hendrix had asked that I meet him in the hospital cafeteria tomorrow at one o'clock, so my night was free. I took a chance and called Sue, my old next-door neighbor.

"Evie, how are you?"

"Hey, Sue. Nice to hear your voice. I'm in town, and was wondering if I could stop by the shop."

"What? You're in town? Yes, that would be great. I am at 555 Cliff Hill."

"Great. See you soon."

The shop was a cute little building, brightly painted with stands filled with flowers outside.

When I walked inside, I saw Sue standing behind the counter, apron on, scissors in hand, creating a beautiful bouquet. Another woman asked if she could help me find something.

"Actually, I am looking for my old neighbor."

Sue turned around and gave me a gigantic smile. "Evie! You made it. Welcome."

"Beautiful little place you have here."

"Thank you. Evie, let me introduce you to the other owner. Mary, this is my old neighbor, Evie. She is the one I told you about who helped me realize that being a florist was my genuine passion."

"So nice to meet you. And thank you. Sue has been an amazing partner. Business is up."

"That's wonderful news. Congratulations to you both."

Sue and I caught up, and I shared some photos of my commissioned piece. It was apparent that Sue was in her element, and it thrilled me. When I left, we hugged, and she gave me a stunning little arrangement that she had just made.

***

I arrived at the cafeteria early and found a quiet table to wait.

My phone rang.

"He loved it!" was the first thing Tatum said when I answered the phone.

"He does?" I exhaled deeply.

"Yes, and he is very excited to receive it. When can you ship it out?"

"Well …" I stammered.

"Evie, what is it?"

"Actually, I'm here in Denver."

"You're here? Why are you here?"

"A special friend needed my help, so I came out unexpectedly."

"And when will you go back?"

"I don't know."

"Hmm … This could be a problem. Wait. I shouldn't say a problem; just something that we will need to figure out."

"Actually, I may have a solution. Give me a day, and I will get back to you."

"Okay, that will give me time to arrange for the pickup and shipping," she replied. "I hope everything is okay, and if you have a chance, I would love to see you."

"I hope everything will be okay, as well."

When I got off the phone with Tatum, I reached out to Steve.

"Steve, huge favor to ask. Please call me."

While waiting for his reply, I just sat and waited for Hendrix. I had never liked hospitals much. I always got a weird feeling. The noises and smells put me on edge. Watching people walk by, I could tell who had just arrived to be with family and friends and those who had been here for a while. The look in their eyes told it all. I saw fear, anxiety, worry, exhaustion. Happily, I could say there were a few where I could see joy. I assumed they must be here for the birth of a baby.

The phone rang, jolting me out of deep thought.

"Steve, thanks for calling so quickly."

"Yeah, what's up? Everything okay?"

"Still working on it, but I need to ask a favor."

"Sure, what is it?"

"I'm back in Colorado. A friend needed my help, and I don't know how long I will be out here. You remember the commissioned piece I was working on?"

"Of course."

"Well, the buyer would like it sooner than originally planned. My agent is making all the arrangements for pickup, but I need someone to be there to ensure that they package it properly."

"Do you know when?"

"Not yet, but I should know in a day or two."

"Okay, just let me know. Maybe I will ask my cousin to help me. That is an enormous responsibility for a non-artist." I could hear the worry in his voice.

"Thank you! I didn't want to ask Granddad."

"I understand. No worries. Just let me know what you need, and I will make it happen."

"You're a lifesaver. Thank you."

After we hung up, I began people watching again. Then I saw him walking over to me, handsome as ever. My heart skipped a beat, but I tried to act nonchalant.

"Thanks for meeting me here," he said as he sat down.

"Of course. How is Aja?"

"She is doing okay. Her treatment is really taking a toll on her, but the big bear brought a smile to her face."

"I'm so glad."

We looked at each other uncomfortably.

Hendrix began, "I don't know where to start. You really surprised me when I saw you yesterday. I didn't know how to deal with all my feelings, so I just shut down."

"Sorry for the surprise, but I knew you wouldn't have asked me to come out, and if I suggested it, you probably wouldn't have wanted me to make the trip. I feel badly about how I reacted to your phone call and news. I was also going through stuff that I didn't want to be doing on my own. In the end, it was better that I had, but I know my words didn't actually say what I wanted them to, and I could tell that I hurt you."

"Well, it seemed like we both were hurtful in how we handled this."

"Hendrix, I know we can't just go back to the way things were. And, in all honesty, it's better that we don't. But I will put it out there that I hope one day we will get to the place that we both hoped we could be together."

"Thanks, Evie. I have a similar hope. But, for now, I need to focus on Aja and my new reality as a father."

When he said father, I felt like I had been hit by a bus. I didn't know what I thought would happen, or even if I had allowed myself to think about anything else, but Hendrix was a father. Anything that he said after that didn't compute.

"Evie, did you hear me? How long will you be staying?"

"Oh, sorry," I mumbled, still not completely back to the present. "I'm here for you as long as you need me."

There was a long, pregnant pause, neither one of us knowing what do next. I longed for him to say that he needed me and didn't want me to leave, but it also scared me. My new life back on the island was what I truly enjoyed. I wanted to go back.

"You hungry?" he asked.

"Yes," I said, a bit too eagerly. Not that I was starving. I just wanted to end this conversation.

After lunch, Hendrix looked at his watch. "Hey, I gotta go. My shift. Aja's mom needs to get back to work."

"I understand. Same time tomorrow?" I asked hesitantly.

"That would be great," Hendrix said with a smile.

***

That night, Tatum and I got together for dinner. It was wonderful to see her and to give her an update on the studio.

"So, how do you feel now that the painting is complete, and you know he loves it?"

"I feel great, but it took a bit of mental work to get here."

"How so?"

"Moving back to the island came with a lot of unknowns. Could I paint? Would they sell? But I also found out that there were many unknowns about my family that had hindered me my whole life. I worked through many of those things, allowing myself to feel the pain and confusion, but to also let it go. I had always thought that I could never please my grandfather. And that doubt crossed over into many facets of my life. It actually made me a workaholic—always trying to be perfect. In the end, all he was trying to do was protect me. I can appreciate that, and now that I understand, I can let it go. Only until I could do that, could I actually paint that picture."

"Remarkable, just remarkable. Now that you say all this, I can understand your painting more, and it gives me a better understanding of you. Evie Prince, you are a powerful person to take on all those emotions and process them in such a way that has allowed you to grow. I am impressed. So, does that mean I will see more paintings?"

"Yes, you will. I heard the island is very quiet in the winter, so I should have a lot of time to paint."

"Wonderful, because my list of interested buyers is growing. I will do a big promotion around this commissioned piece. I am happy to say you have just elevated yourself into a whole new area of the art world."

Hearing Tatum say that was almost more than I could handle. I had craved this type of success for so long, and now that it was here, I didn't know what to do.

In the back of my head, I heard, *"Enjoy it!"*

I put my head down and let out a little giggle.

"What's so funny?"

"My higher self just told me to enjoy it, so I guess that is what I will do."

***

For the rest of the week, Hendrix and I met for lunch. It was wonderful spending time with him, learning about Aja and helping him manage his feelings. As the week came to a close, though, we both knew it was time for me to get back.

Our last lunch, words were scarce. Neither one of us wanted to say the inevitable goodbye. We promised each other to talk as often as possible, but we would for sure check in once a week.

"Thank you for taking this time and being with me. I couldn't have gotten through this week without you."

"Gee whiz," I replied in a teasing voice. "In all seriousness. You would have managed just fine. I'm glad that I could take a little of the weight off your shoulders. Aja is going to be fine and grow up to be a beautiful woman. She is lucky to have you as her father. And I look forward to meeting her one day when this is all over."

"Evie, thank you. I would invite you to meet her, but ..." He trailed off.

"Hendrix, please, you and I both know that time will come when it is right."

"At least let me send you a picture of her and the bear. She adores it. When she saw it, she gave me the biggest smile. The biggest one since she has been in here."

"I would love that. Thank you." I stood to leave, and Hendrix also stood and met my gaze. He opened his arms, and I gladly accepted his big, warm hug. His smell took me to another time and place. I didn't want to let go, but I had to.

As I pulled away, he looked down at me as if he wanted to kiss me. We both smiled, knowing that it was better that we didn't.

Walking away from him was hard, but I knew in my heart that this was only a pause in our relationship. When we came back together, we would be stronger than we would have been if this had never happened.

CHAPTER 8 — PROFESSIONAL ARTIST

I pulled into the driveway just in time to meet Steve and his cousin, Beth.

"Thank you both for your willingness to help me. I didn't think I would make it back in time."

"Not a problem at all. This gives me the opportunity to see your work. Steve has been raving about this piece, so I was excited to have the chance to view it for myself," Beth explained.

I led them both to the studio and opened the door. In the middle of the room was the piece. Admittedly, I was startled by the enormity of the painting. It was great to see it one last time before it got shipped off.

"Oh, Evie, this is spectacular," Beth said with a gasp.

Steve stood there with this told-you-so look on his face.

"The colors and transition of light are almost"—she paused—"spiritual."

I blushed, not knowing what to say, but then I reminded myself to accept the compliment openly and without judgment. "Thank you."

"So, Evie, have you had a showing yet?"

"No, not yet. I really don't have enough paintings to host a showing. Each time I have painted a piece, I have sold it, and this was a commissioned piece. I hoped to have time this winter to get more paintings under my belt to host a showing next summer."

"Well, congratulations. Your work is beautiful. I will have another showing around Christmastime and would love you to show some of your work, as well, if you are open to it."

"Seriously? That would be amazing!"

In the background, we could hear a truck rumbling up the road.

"Right on time," I announced as two young men jumped out of the truck.

Steve looked at one and said, "Peter? Is that you?"

"Hey, Steve. Nice to see you, man. What have you been up to?"

"Just working, keeping my nose clean, and hanging with these two artistic types, hoping their talent will rub off on me," he said jokingly.

"Glad to hear life is good. Keep up the good work."

"Yeah, life is fantastic. Thanks. Now, be careful with this," Steve warned. "It is very special."

The men worked quickly, and I tried to keep my mouth shut as to not make them more nervous. When it was all said and done, I let out a tremendous sigh of relief and texted Tatum, giving her the status.

"Geez, Steve, you know everyone," I kidded.

"Not everyone, but almost," he replied with a smile. "Peter was just leaving the program when I started. He was a really nice guy and would always say, *stay strong*."

"And he has," Beth replied proudly.

"Yes, he has."

We all turned to see Granddad at the door.

"What? Did my invitation get lost in the mail? Glad to see you back here, kid. How was your trip?"

"It was good. A lot to share."

"Well, I look forward to hearing about it. Beth, nice to see you. How have you been?"

"Wonderful. As you know, life is good."

"I see you have been keeping Steve in line. You must be exhausted," Granddad teased.

"Ha-ha. You know I can hear you, right?" Steve retorted.

"Nothing but love, young man, nothing but love.

"So, Evie. How do you want to celebrate this wonderful achievement?"

"A lobster dinner works for me."

"Can do. Steve, Beth, I hear there is a little bistro right through the bushes that serves a mean blue-plate lobster special. Want to join?"

"Who can pass up lobster?" both Beth and Steve said in unison, and then we all laughed.

After dinner, we sat around, telling stories. Steve seemed to be the brunt of many of them.

I turned to Steve. "Were you serious when you said you're interested in art?"

Steve shifted in his seat, looking a little uncomfortable. "I have thought about it."

"So, what are you going to do about it?" Granddad asked.

"Hang around Beth and Evie and hope their talent rubs off on me," he replied in a cheeky manner.

"No, seriously, Steve, you want to be an artist?" Beth asked. "You never told me that."

"Well, it's a little daunting when your cousin is so amazing. And now my new friend is equally amazing. Can't say that I'm ready to jump into the fray and be compared to the likes of you two."

"Who says you will be compared?" I probed. "We all have gifts, and we are all meant to share those gifts. One is not better than the other. I would be happy to teach you what I know. My grandmother taught me how to paint right over there, out on the deck. Now I have a studio that you so expertly built for me. It's all I could do to pay back your generosity. You game?"

We all looked at Steve as he contemplated the offer. I thought he waited a little longer for dramatic effect.

"Yes, I'm game."

"Wonderful! We can start tomorrow after you finish work."

"Well, I don't know about that." He hesitated.

"Come on, Steve. What else do you have to do, other than be over at that fire house?" Granddad challenged.

"Fine. I will see you tomorrow." And, with that, Steve said his goodnights.

"Well, I guess we are done," Beth commented. "Attaquin, it has been a pleasure, as always."

After they left, I helped Granddad clean up.

"Hey, kid, I'm proud of you. I know it took a lot to finish that painting."

"Yes, there were a lot of emotions that I had to process, but it needed to happen. Thank you for being there for me."

"So, what happened out in Denver? I assume you and Hendrix are good."

"It was an interesting trip. We're good, but we are not the same. We talked it out and agreed that Hendrix has a lot to manage now with Aja's illness and him being a father. I like to think we have just hit the pause button."

"What is meant to be will be."

"Thanks, Granddad, I believe that, as well."

When I got back to my place, the exhaustion hit me. I collapsed into bed and told my grandparents that I had finally done it. I had become a professional artist.

Knowing the pride that they felt for me put me in a wonderful space. This was the feeling that I had desired for so long. But now I knew it wasn't their approval or pride that was important; it was my own.

Drifting off to sleep, I heard my phone ping. Whatever it was, it could wait.

***

OMG, she was beautiful. Her eyes sparkled, her skin glowed, and those curls … Oh, she was so frigging cute, and I could see a bit of Hendrix in her.

I replied to Hendrix.

"Thank you for the sunshine to start my day. Aja is absolutely beautiful."

CHAPTER 9 — SHARE YOUR LIGHT

Around seven o'clock, I heard Steve coming up the road and met him out front.

"Glad to see you. I was wondering if you were still coming."

"Yup, sorry it's so late. Got caught up at work."

"I'm just happy that you made it," I told him as we headed up to sit on the deck. "So, my plan was to teach you how my grandmother taught me, plus a little something-something that I picked up along the way. Sound good?"

"Yup, I'm following so far."

"So, tell me why you want to paint."

"Honestly, I'm looking for an outlet. I still have so many emotions caught up inside of me. Staying clean is a daily focus. When something angers or frustrates me, I have to remember that it needs to be processed. I can't hide and bury my head in alcohol. I need to feel it and deal with it. Sometimes, it feels like it can be too much, and I get tempted."

I bow my head, trying to hide my smile.

"Why are you smiling?" Steve asked, not even trying to hide his dismay.

"I understand what you're feeling. My addiction was trying to be perfect and successful. Always trying to make someone else proud rather than myself. I also use painting to express my feelings, to get out the angst, to express love, and to remember.

Since we agree, let's start with the something-something that has taken my painting ability to the next level." I looked out at the lighthouse in the distance and revealed, "My higher self guides me in every painting."

"You mean, your gut?"

"You could call it that. It's the energy that tells you deep down if something feels good or bad. I call it my higher self. Some people call it God. For you, it's your gut. Whatever you call it, you should always remember to make time to listen to it."

"'Kay, still following."

"For me, inspiration generally comes from an experience. I associate my paintings with the energy or emotion that I felt at that moment. I allow myself to feel it again as vividly as I can, then I put brush to canvas, not knowing what will emerge. Sometimes it is beautiful, other times it is ugly, but it is always my truth.

"My grandmother painted for years. She was amazing, but it was only at the end of her physical life that she painted her truth. Those are the most stunning paintings I have ever seen." I looked over at Steve and noticed his eyes were misty. "Everything okay?"

"Yeah, everything is wonderful. I feel like I have found my place, and I haven't even lifted a brush yet." He paused, took a deep breath, and then looked me straight in the eyes. "I don't want to get all woo, woo weird on you, but do you know how powerful you are? Just sitting here with you, listening to your words, was like my consciousness just filled with light, and when I look at you, light surrounds you. Wow, that was crazy. I have never felt that before."

Steve's words shook me, but then I remembered the time Colbie and I sat down after I lost my job. The energy she exuded had been magical.

"Hey, wait here," I told him as I went inside to grab one of my grandmother's paintings. When I came back, I handed it to him. "This is what I am talking about."

"Geez. I have never seen anything like that before. It's extraordinary."

"This is my grandmother painting her true self. Just know that you can do it, as well."

Steve and I sat in silence, reflecting on Grandma's painting.

"Well, why don't we call it a night?" I suggested.

"Sounds good."

"Tomorrow, we will play with paint."

For the next week, Steve came over every night. I showed him how to mix paints, brush usage, various paint strokes, and a bunch of other stuff. After that first week, we took a week off so that he could do his own experimenting.

Working with Steve gave me the energy to paint myself. Inspiration was everywhere—walks on the beach, driving down island, stuck behind a moped, watching the sunset. I felt energy all around me, and I painted freely. I painted just for myself. Some were good, some were better than good, and some were just bad. No judgment. They were all mine, and I had fun painting every one of them.

***

"Hey, can I come by tonight? I have something to show you."

"Sure. If I'm not here, I am over at Granddad's."

"Great. It won't be too late."

At eight o'clock, I heard Steve come up the road. I had just gotten back from dinner with Granddad, and I was settling in for the night.

"Knock, knock. Evie, you home?"

"Yup, be right there. Come on in."

When I walked out into the living room, I saw Steve with a brown, wrapped package. "Whatcha got?"

Steve held out the package. "For you."

"What?" I took the package from him and brought it to the kitchen table. I could feel Steve's eyes on my every movement.

I was being really careful with the packaging when he blurted out, "Will you open it already!"

"Okay, okay." Then I saw it, and an enormous smile crossed my face.

"You like it?"

"I love it. It's fantastic!"

"The inspiration was the emotion I felt the night out on the deck when you shared the something-something with me."

"Steve, thank you. How did you feel painting it?"

"A warm, tingly feeling overwhelmed me. I don't really remember the painting process, but when I was done, I felt at peace."

"You have just given me so much joy. This is what my grandmother must have felt when she taught me. It feels wonderful. Thank you. Where should I hang it?"

"Oh, whoa, you want to hang it? For others to see?"

"Yes, and I hope you signed it. I want to say that I knew you when."

"Ha-ha, whatever. Hey, Evie, have you ever thought about teaching others your gift? You know, like teaching a class? They are always looking for people in the community to bring their expertise to the high school."

"Teach? I don't know about that."

"I have friends down there. Just let me know. Things get quiet around here in the winter. It may break up the monotony."

"Thanks for the compliment. I have never thought of myself as a teacher."

"Remember, you said that we all need to share our gift. Painting is yours. I'm just saying …"

"Touché. I will think about it."

***

Once I got settled in bed, I sent Hendrix a text. We hadn't spoken most of the week, so I wanted to make sure that he and Aja were doing okay.

"*Just checking in on you. Hope everything is going as good as can be expected. Sending you and Aja healing energy.*"

Not more than a few minutes later, he responded.

"*How is that you always know when I need your energy? So good to hear from you. Can I call?*"

"*Please.*"

I picked up on the first ring. "Is everything okay?"

"Yes, Aja is responding to her treatments. We hope she will only need one more round."

"That is amazing news. How are you holding up?"

"Now that Aja is doing better, her mother is trying to push me away. I don't understand."

"Seems like it scares her that she has to share Aja with you. Didn't you say you would not have known you had a daughter but for the fact that her mother couldn't pay for the treatments?"

"Yes, but I'm not trying to take her away. I just want her in my life now."

"I'm going to remind you of what you have told me. Look at this situation through the eyes of love. It will make things look different."

"Evie, thank you. Thank you for being here for me."

"I love you, Hendrix Talisman. How could I not be there for you?"

Hendrix let out a long sigh. "Evie, to hear you say that feels incredible. Like a big, warm hug. I have always known that you love me, but now I know that you also love yourself, I am so proud of you."

"Thank you. I am really proud of me, too!"

CHAPTER 10 — NYC

"*Come to the City. I miss your face,*" was Reva's text to me. She had an unconventional style, but you always knew where you stood with her.

It had been a few months since she and Brian had gotten engaged. Both of our lives had finally settled down, and it was time we had a girls' weekend. Back in the day, I would have jumped on a plane without a second thought, but I lived a more modest life now. So, I took the boat and reserved a seat on Peter Pan and Megabus. They would be my chauffeurs for my trip to the big city.

Seven plus hours later, we pulled into New York City. The ride wasn't too bad.

As we had gotten closer, I could feel the energy grow with more people, the smells, the noise, and lights. When I walked out of the station, I looked up immediately and just took it all in. The awe quickly dissipated as someone bumped me since I was standing in the middle of the sidewalk. *Geez, Evie, you look like a tourist.* I had to remember my city etiquette.

For as busy as the city was, it was still quieter than before the pandemic.

I had a couple of hours before Reva was done with work, so I slowly made my way to her apartment over in Brooklyn. Once I got my bearings, I moved through the city with ease. It had been so long since I had been here that I was seeing the little things around me—the people, the diversity, the amazing and not so amazing smells. Stimuli surrounded me. Just a few short years ago, I wouldn't have noticed a thing. My impatience and ego had kept me blind to all the beauty. Now, I saw fall in the city, and it was amazing.

Sitting on the steps of Reva's brownstone, I watched as the world passed by. Then, in the distance, I heard, "Girl, you made it."

When I stood up, I saw Reva strutting down the sidewalk, looking fabulous. I jumped off the steps and ran over to give her a hug. A big, warm hug.

"Girl, it is so good to see you. You look so relaxed and happy," Reva said, eyeing me up and down.

"And you have a glow that lights up the street," I responded.

"Gee, thanks." Reva blushed. "I will admit that I have never been happier. Come on; let's get inside."

Inside, I made myself comfortable. This was my home away from home.

"The place looks good. You've made some changes."

"Yes, I needed to make room for Brian's things."

"So, he is moving here?"

"Actually, we haven't decided. I was hoping we could hunker down for the weekend and just talk. There are so many things going through my head, and I am just trying to figure things out."

"I hear you. Laying low sounds wonderful."

We both changed into our sweats, ordered in, and got comfy. Thirty minutes later, the food was at the door. How I missed Ethiopian food. We ordered the meat and veggie plate for two and jumped right in.

"I wuv this stuff," I said with a full mouth.

Reva nodded.

It wasn't until we almost finished the plate before we took a breath.

"So, how is wedding planning going?"

"Slow. We can't decide if we want to go big or intimate."

"How intimate? Eloping intimate?"

"Maybe."

"Is that what you want?"

"You know I'm not big into the white wedding stuff. Never have been. But Brian feels like they expect it of us."

"From whom?"

"His family."

"Hasn't he already been married?"

"Yes, years ago."

"I guess the question you have to ask yourself is: who's the wedding for?"

"What do you mean?"

"Are you having a wedding for you and Brian or for his family?"

"For us, of course."

"Then do what you want. To me, a commitment to your partner is a very intimate thing, be it formal and legal or a promise. Why bring other's expectations into it? You are both grown; do what you want. And if you want a big wedding, then have one, but do it for you and him, not anyone else."

"What are you and Hendrix going to do?"

"We are a long way from that, but I would think the same way."

"What do you mean, *you are a long way from that*?"

"I will keep it short, and we can discuss it later, but we are taking a pause."

"I'm sorry."

"No need. It's what we need."

"Whatever Brian and I decide, will you stand with me?"

"Absolutely!"

After a few glasses of wine, we reminisced the ups and downs of our lives and how we were finally getting to the place we wanted to be.

"Evie, every time I see you, you look different. Younger."

"I feel like I am continually changing. I'm learning to love myself, doing things I would have never thought I could do. Actually living and creating my life, not just being a bystander, watching my life. It feels good."

"Well, it shows."

***

I woke early to the sounds of the City. *Toto, we are not on the Vineyard anymore.*

I snuck outside and sat on the stairs, taking in the cool morning. Meditation was a little harder with the sights and sounds, but I managed to quiet my mind. Then, as I turned to go back inside, Reva was coming out the door with two cups of coffee.

"I knew you would be out here."

"Setting my intentions for the day."

"Nice. I need to do that more often. I get so caught up sometimes that I don't even stop to hear what I want; I just do as I've done before."

"Is it time to get out of the City? Change things up?"

"It may be, but I never thought I would live in Philly."

"Who says you have to live there? Why can't you find a new place? A place for just you two?"

"That would be wonderful, but his job."

"*Blah, blah, blah.* Practice what you preach, Reva. Remember, I was in a similar place not that long ago."

"Yes, you were, and you made it work."

"So, why can't you?"

"I just don't know where Brian is in all of this."

"Seems like that is a discussion that you should have, right?"

"Right. It is always so good to talk with you, Evie. You remind me that I can create my life."

"That is something that I try to remind myself of every day—listen to my heart, and I *am* the creator of my life."

We ate ourselves through the rest of the weekend. I tried to have everything that I knew I would not get for a while.

"Evie, you are going to make yourself sick. You know you can visit anytime."

"I know, but I wuv Greek," I added between bites.

"Hey, how is Attaquin doing?"

"He is wonderful. It is so nice having him in my life. He was always special to me, but to know I have him as family is extra special."

"Have you asked him much about your indigenous side?"

"Huh? No, I haven't, really. I've been so busy learning about my grandparents and working through those feelings that I had thought little about it."

"Don't let that wait too long." She looked at me with knowing eyes.

Reva's life had been far from easy. She had separated herself from the family that had, and would continue, to do her harm, if allowed. There was one person who got her through all the hard times, and that had been her great-aunt, Rosa. I had only met her a few times, but she was like granddad—the salt of the earth. She would tell you like it was and didn't mince words. Thinking about it, Reva's personality was just like hers. Unfortunately, Reva had never gotten the opportunity to truly learn about her aunt and her life. In Reva's mind, her aunt Rosa was her genuine mother, and I was her sister from a different mister. Now, I was her only family.

***

"Thank you for coming to visit. I just needed to slow down and have Reva/Evie time."

"Anything for my sister."

"Ah, shucks. Be careful going back and text me when you are on the bus." Reva gave me an enormous hug then ran out the door. I heard her clomping down the stairs and looked out the window right as she went out the door. She looked up and blew me a kiss.

I had a few hours before my bus reservation, so I got dressed, packed my bag, and straightened up. My intention was to walk as far as I could before I had to take a train back to the bus station.

Walking the streets and taking in the sights gave me so much inspiration. I wanted to bottle all of this emotion up so I had it when I got back to the island.

The bus station was filled with people from all walks of life. Some just passing through, some arriving for the first time, and some just trying to get out. It was a delightful visit, but I was happy to leave it behind and return to my little island.

CHAPTER 11 — WAMPUM

People were not kidding when they said that the island slowed down in the winter. All the college kids were back at school, shops were shutting down, and the island was getting back to normal.

Today was shopping day. I needed to buy some new paints, food, and pick up a few things for Granddad. The trip down island took no time. People knew where they were going. Everyone seemed to smile more and wanted to say hello.

Walking out of the market, I ran into Mr. Frank.

"Hey, Evie. How was your summer?"

"Hi, Mr. Frank. It was busy but good."

"Hear you built yourself an art studio."

It surprised me that he knew, but not really. Word traveled fast on the island. "Yes, I did. It's beautiful."

"So, Steve tells me you would be interested in teaching painting classes at the high school."

I laughed. "Well, I told him I would think about it."

"I hope you do. We are always looking for locals to bring their expertise into the school. We want the kids to know that there are so many paths that they can take. After the holidays would be a great time to come in. If you commit within the next month, we can get you on the schedule."

"It sounds good, but I have never worked with kids before. I don't know if I could teach them."

"Ha, if you can inspire Steve, I am sure you will be fine."

"Can you give me a week to think about it?"

"Sure can. Did Steve do well by you on your road?"

"Huh? What do you mean?"

"Just wanted to make sure he did a good job."

"Yes, he did a great job. How did you know about the road?"

"I was the one who contracted him to do it."

"I'm sorry—you did what?"

"I hired Steve to fix your road."

"But, why? I mean, thank you … but why?"

"Your dad and I were good friends, and he asked that I look out for you."

"Oh, you mean my granddad, Attaquin Brown."

"No, I mean your father, Paul Brown."

I stopped dead in my tracks, and my heart dropped. "You knew my father? Why didn't you tell me?"

"He asked that I didn't. After your mother died, he made me promise to look out for you at the high school and …"

"And what? How is it I am the last person to know my own flesh and blood? I'm sorry, Mr. Frank, but when will this end? Is there anything else I should know?"

"He loved you deeply, and he was sorry that he could not be the father that he knew you needed."

"Sorry to ask this, but did he love my mother, or was I a oops baby?"

"Wow. Yes, he loved your mother deeply. He tried to be a husband and father, but …"

"Demons."

"Yes, he had too many demons that he just couldn't escape from. He regularly asked how you were doing in school. He was so proud of you."

"This is a lot for me to handle right now, Mr. Frank, and I don't know if I'm in the right place to manage it. So, I am going to leave, but I hope that, in time, when I'm ready, you will tell me more about my father."

"Of course. I apologize, Evie, for springing this on you like that. Once I heard you knew Attaquin was your grandfather, I just assumed."

"Don't apologize. Thank you, Mr. Frank, for your generosity and for watching out for me back when I was in school. You really were my only friend."

***

When I got back up island, I dropped my stuff at the house then headed right over to Granddad's.

"Come on in."

"Got your stuff."

"Thanks. Was it busy down island?"

"No, not bad at all, but I ran into Mr. Frank, my old math teacher from high school." I paused to see if Granddad showed any reaction.

Nothing.

"Guess what?" I said.

"What?"

"Mr. Frank was the person who paid to have the road fixed."

"Why would he do that?"

"He said he was a good friend of Dad's and that he promised to look out for me. That is also why he was so nice to me in high school."

"Hmm … let me see something." Granddad went into his bedroom then brought out an old high school yearbook, flipping through the pages. "Here he is—Bill Frank." He handed me the book.

It was hard to tell, but I could see that it was Mr. Frank under all that hair. "He wrote something to Dad."

Remember, I got your back. ALWAYS!

"Short, but I remember Bill was on the quiet side."

"Do you remember them hanging out much?"

"Not that I remember, but your father was always going down island. People never come up island unless they lived here or wanted to look at the cliffs. Well, you had a hell of a day so far."

I nodded in agreement. "Tell me about it."

"When you're ready, look in the trunk. There you should find a small silk pouch. That was from your father."

I just looked at Granddad. "Seriously, I don't know how much more I can take."

"You said you wanted to know."

"And I do."

"When you're ready."

I got up and headed back to my house, mind swirling. Still so much for me to learn.

I crashed on the couch, exhausted from all the emotions of the day, and fell asleep.

Two hours later, I woke to a sharp pain in my foot. I didn't know what bit me, but my foot was swelling up.

"Hello?"

"Granddad, something bit me, and my foot is swelling up. Do you have any Benadryl?"

"Sorry, kid, I don't. Let me call over to the firehouse to see if anyone is over there. They would have something."

Less than fifteen minutes, I heard a truck coming up the road. It was Steve with his EMT kit.

Bang, bang. "Evie, you there?"

"Yup, I'm here, on the couch. Come on in."

"Holy shit, would you look at that? What bit you?"

"I have no idea. I fell asleep on the couch, and I woke up to a sharp pain in my foot. Then it just started blowing up."

"Are you allergic to anything?"

"Not that I know of."

"Okay, take some of this antihistamine. Hopefully, this will help."

Steve sat with me until the swelling went down.

"Guess who I saw down island today?" I asked.

"Who?"

"Mr. Frank, from the high school."

"Really?"

"Yes, and he told me."

"Okay, good. I'm not very good at lying."

"Seems like my life is still filled with so many secrets."

"Evie, don't think you are the only one. Everyone has secrets. That's why I started drinking—trying to hide from secrets. At least you are dealing with these things. If not, you could be in a lot of worse places."

My foot finally went back to normal size, and we could see the spot where I had been bitten.

"I would say, if your foot swells again, or if you don't feel well tomorrow, you should probably go down to the emergency room."

"Thanks, Steve, I appreciate the help."

"Of course. So, are you going to teach the art class? I really think you should."

"I told him to give me a week to decide."

"All right. Give a call if you need anything."

"Will do, and thanks."

***

"*I need you*," flashed across my phone screen.

I put my brush down and called Hendrix. "What's up? Is Aja okay?"

"I don't know. Her mother is not returning my phone calls. I don't know what to do."

"Breathe is what you need to do. When was the last time you spoke with her?"

"A couple of days ago. We were planning for me to take Aja for an overnight, to give her mother a break. Then, when I called to solidify the plans, she didn't answer the phone. I called multiple times, leaving messages, but nothing."

"Do you know her family? Can you reach out to them to see if everything is okay?"

"I did, but they haven't heard from her, either. Evie, I can't lose Aja."

"Hendrix, close your eyes and breathe. Inhale peace and exhale anxiety. Keep on breathing." I could feel his energy become less frantic. "Now that you are calm, ask your higher self what you should do."

We sat in silence for a few minutes.

"I am guided to call her again, but this time to let her know that I know she is scared, that I am not trying to take Aja away from her, and that I am here for her."

"Good. That is really good. Looking at the situation through the eyes of love."

Hendrix chuckled. "Oh, how the roles have changed. Once upon a time, I said that to you, and now you are reminding me."

"I told you I am here for you. Call me anytime, if for nothing else but to sit on the phone together."

"I love you, Evie Prince."

"And I love you, Hendrix Talisman."

After we hung up, I sat in my studio, daydreaming of what it would have been like to have my father in my life and how lucky Aja was to have a father like Hendrix. A wave of emotion overcame me, and I realized for the first time how hard it must have been for him to be out of my life, to watch me from a far, and to make the conscious decision to never let me know who he was.

I cleaned up my paints, went back into the house, and grabbed the trunk key from the windowsill. When I opened the trunk, I had one purpose—to find the silk pouch. Normally, I was overly cautious when I looked through the trunk. This time, I pulled everything out, needing to find that silk pouch. Finally, in a small bundle of baby clothes, I found it.

The pouch was a small, yellow embroidered bag with a snap closure. I opened it carefully then pulled out a tiny wampum bracelet. It was beautiful. I held it in my hand and cried. I cried for the love that I felt in that bracelet. Cried for not knowing my father. Cried for the sacrifice that he had made for me.

***

"Granddad, I want to know everything about my father."

"I see you found the bracelet that he made you."

"Yes, and it is beautiful."

He took a deep breath. "Well, for me to tell you about your father, I need to tell you about this side of your family. We are the people of the first light and have inhabited this area for ten thousand years. Our tribe was brought to this land by a great being named Moshup. Tired from his travels, Moshup dragged his toe across the land, creating a small channel that separated this area from the mainland. The channel filled with water and grew larger with the ocean tides, creating this island, Martha's Vineyard or, in our language, Noepe.

"We were the first inhabitants of this island, and many of us continued to live here. In the beginning, we lived all over the island. We had three bands of our tribe that called this island home. We traded with the people from the far north. They were peaceful, and they always returned to their home.

"When the Pilgrims came, they did not leave, causing our people and our sister tribes throughout New England great harm. They brought disease and a belief system that classified us as savages. We were killed or captured and made into slaves. It was genocide, plain and simple.

"Throughout history, we suffered. For some, they could not overcome that trauma—always considered a lesser being, having our land and traditions desecrated, being told we are being honored when, in reality, we are being denigrated. Asked to fight in wars to protect this land that we inhabited before anyone else, but when we return home, not being acknowledged for our sacrifice.

"I tell you all these things because these are the demons that your father carried with him. He could not find joy in his time on this earth, feeling the pain of our ancestors. He watched and experienced the discrimination and humiliation, but this was not his path. He was filled with anger and punished himself every day for not being able to live as they expected him in this world.

"Your mother saw his light, felt his struggles, but she knew he was not meant for this world.

"When you were born, he felt genuine joy for the first time. He saw himself in your eyes. This made him proud, but it also frightened him." Granddad hung his head, holding back the tears. "Your father tried his best, but he knew he was not meant to be in your life. He watched over you the best he could and asked others to do the same when he knew he could not."

As Granddad softly sobbed, I took his hand and held it.

"I miss my boy every day. He was a part of me, but I feel him often, and he longs for you to be open to him so that you may feel his energy, as well."

"Granddad, I did. I felt his love when I held the bracelet. It was so powerful."

"His energy is powerful. He is your protector. He has always been, and will always be, there for you."

Before I left, I gave Granddad a huge hug and, for the first time, he felt frail in my arms. If he were not the man that he was, I believed my father's passing would have killed him. No wonder Granddad has helped so many, pouring the love and energy that he had for his son into those who he knew he could help.

I slipped back through the bushes and headed straight for the studio. I had so much loving energy pumping through me, and I needed to capture it on canvas.

My bracelet served as inspiration. The surge of love that I experienced when I held it. The perfect beads made from shell. White transforming into light purple then to deep, dark purple. The love that I felt for a man who I never knew. Purple, beautiful shades of purple, expressed this love on the canvas. Purple to represent the significance of the wampum but also the crown chakra—the spiritual connection to the divine and to my father.

When it was completed, I felt like it had opened a new door within me. I could feel the energy around me like I had never felt it before. My head tingled, goosebumps on my arms, a hum in the air. I was fully present, if only for a moment. I was perfectly in the now.

This one was for Granddad, to remind him of the love and energy that his son, Paul Brown, gave to him every moment of every day.

CHAPTER 12 — NOR'EASTER

Fall on the island was perfect. It was quiet, the weather was cool, and I got to wear all my favorite sweaters and coats.

Painting became my pastime. Tatum had been thrilled with my progress, and I had been regularly selling pieces. The press that I had received for the commissioned piece had really launched my career internationally. I had also been honing my teaching skills as I committed to teaching a painting class at the high school. Teaching was new to me, but I couldn't imagine it being much different than running a sales team … I hoped.

Today, the weather was strange. A bit overcast. Granddad said that we could be in for a storm, a real Nor'easter. I watched little television, so I wasn't keeping up with the storm's path.

"Hey, kid, you in there?"

"Yup."

Granddad walked into the kitchen. "Have you filled your bathtub yet?"

I looked at him strangely. "Why would I do that?"

"Looks like we're going to get hit by the storm later today or tomorrow. Better fill it up. Do you have food?"

"Yes, I just went shopping the other day."

"How about candles and flashlights?"

"Yup, got those when I first moved here."

"Good. Then you should be ready. Make sure you bring in anything from outside that you don't want to get thrown around. I'm headed out to secure the boat. Want to come?"

"Sure."

We jumped into his truck and headed down to the water. Everyone and his brother were there, tying and securing their boats.

"Attaquin, need any help?" a young man yelled over our way.

"Thanks, Jeffery, but we're good. Looks like she's heading our way earlier than expected. The water's as flat as piss on a board," Granddad announced.

Everyone looked up from what they were doing, noticing how calm the water had gotten, and then they moved quicker.

When we finished, Granddad helped a few others secure their boats, and then we all headed out to get home.

"Want to have some dinner and ride out the Nor'easter with your granddad?"

"That sounds good. Let me go home and grab a few things, and I will be right back."

Granddad had salted cod, boiled potatoes, and some salt pork ready when I got back. My contribution was beer and half a pie that I had purchased the other day.

Dinner was wonderful, and the company was even better. Then we pulled out the cards after we cleaned the dishes and played Gin Rummy.

"Granddad, who was my grandmother?" I asked as I shuffled the cards.

A warm smile crossed his face. "She was a pretty little Narragansett woman named Clara. Stole my heart the first time

I laid eyes on her. Met right out of high school, and we married before I enlisted. She got pregnant with your father right before I shipped out."

"How come I never met her?"

"Oh, you did, when you were first born. But her stay on this earth was shorter than I wanted. Clara had a difficult pregnancy and delivery, but she delivered a healthy, sturdy boy. Her health slowly diminished after that. I got to have her for twenty more years, but it was her time to move on."

"I'm sorry."

"Don't feel sorry for me. I had a wonderful life with Clara. It's not always about the amount of time you spend with someone; it's about the quality of that time. She was perfect for me. We felt joy and sorrow. She was my partner, and I thanked her every day for the light that she gave to me and our son. If I had to do it again, I wouldn't have changed a thing."

"Wow, I hope I will experience that kind of love."

"If you choose to have it, you will. Remember, you are the creator of your world."

"So, did you proclaim you wanted to meet the love of your life?"

"No, not exactly. Unbeknownst to me, I met a woman who loved herself as much as she loved me and others. After the war, all I asked the Creator for was peace and joy, and that is what I got. Don't get me wrong, I have experienced heartache, but it is hard to know what true joy is if you have not felt the other side." Granddad smiled at me then announced, "Gin."

"*Ugh*, how did you do that?"

The wind picked up, and the lights flickered.

"Well, here she comes."

Just as soon as Granddad said that, the lights went out. Sitting there in the dark, I reflected on how nice it was being here with him. I was at peace.

***

Winter came quickly. I had forgotten how cold it got here in the winter. It was a damp cold, unlike Denver, where you could have a foot of snow on the ground and it was still dry. I could never figure out how that worked.

The holidays were upon us, and I was getting my pieces ready for Beth's studio event. I had chosen three of my smaller paintings to show. The dragon fly, one I had done after returning from my trip to New York, and a piece that highlighted the frustration of driving behind a moped. I also had note cards created, hoping that could get my name out there more.

Hendrix and I had been speaking more. He had worked things out with Ajas's mother, and Aja was in complete remission. He was planning a big holiday for his little girl.

"So, what are you getting Aja for your first Christmas with her?"

"Everything she wants," he replied with a huge smile on his face.

"Oh, so you're going to spoil her?"

"Just this once."

"Uh-huh," I said, knowing full well that she had this man wrapped around her little finger.

"Are you ready for the show?" He changed the subject.

"Yes, I have three pieces. Beth's show, from what I heard, is the place to be for art enthusiast. So, hopefully, this will help me make a name for myself here on the island."

"Your work speaks for itself. I wouldn't worry about that too much. Did I tell you that anyone who comes to my house always comments on your painting? These are not art enthusiasts; they are just people who feel, and they can feel the emotion that you put into your paintings."

"Thank you for that. This will be the first time that I'm in a room where people will openly comment on my work. I have always had one or two people comment, but not complete strangers."

"Don't worry. Remember, if they don't like it, that's on them, not you. So, what do you want for Christmas?"

"Joy, peace, and to live up to my full potential."

"Huh, I don't know if I can get that on Amazon and have it shipped in time," Hendrix replied with a chuckle.

"Oh, you mean from you?" I teased. "Nothing. Your presence in my life is all that I need. And you? What can Santa Evie bring you?"

"You already gave it to me."

"What?"

"Your love."

I blushed. *How does that man do that?* I think to myself.

"Actually, I have a surprise for you. Let's do a Zoom call next week. Wear your most festive outfit. It will be official with a Zoom invite and everything."

"*Ooo*, this sounds exciting. I can't wait."

***

When I got to Beth's, her studio was lit up with small, white twinkle lights, creating an ambiance that was warm but elegant. Her paintings hung perfectly, like a museum, with individual lamps that illuminated the details.

"Hey, Evie. Ready for tonight?"

"I think so. Hoping I can handle the criticism."

"I wouldn't worry too much about that. Your work is fantastic, and I am sure that everyone will agree with me. You said you had three paintings, correct?"

"Yes."

"Great. Why don't you set up over here?"

"I also made some note cards that people can take with my contact information."

"Wonderful idea. Less work for me to do when everyone asks me for your contact information," Beth replied with a grin. "Oh, I gotta meet the caterers. Be right back."

I looked over and saw Celeste coming through the door with platters of food.

"Celeste, what are you doing here?"

"Catering this event."

"Are you the caterer?"

"Yup, my first gig. Sorry I haven't been around much. I decided I wanted to be my own boss, so life has been busy getting my business set up, but here I am."

"Congratulations."

"Same to you on the showing. People are going to love you."

Art lovers filled the studio, each one milling around with wine in hand. I felt out of place, but I tried to keep a smile on my face. Granddad and Steve arrived, and I welcomed them both with an enormous hug.

"Whoa. You okay, kid?" Granddad looked at me with concern.

"Yes, just feeling a little nervous."

"I could tell; you almost squished me to death."

Steve didn't know how to respond. This was the first time I ever hugged him.

He tried to hide his surprise by saying, "Don't worry, Evie; everything will be just fine. Can I get you something to drink?"

"Yes! Thank you."

When Steve walked away, Beth brought over an older woman who was showing interest in my paintings.

"Evie, I would like you to meet Eloise. Eloise, this is Evie Prince, the artist."

"Oh, Evie, so very nice to meet you. Please, dear, tell me about this hummingbird painting. I just adore it."

I gave Beth a smile then walked Eloise back over to the painting. As I explained the day that I had experienced the hummingbird, Steve slipped in and gave me my drink. I turned to him and gave him an appreciative smile.

Eloise looked at Steve and commented, "Your husband is very handsome."

I blushed. Then, in unison, Steve and I said, "Oh no, we're just friends."

Eloise leaned in and whispered, "Well, hold tight to that one."

Throughout the evening, Beth introduced me to many other guests. This was the most social interaction that I had had in over two years. It was both tiring and exhilarating. Mostly, people enjoyed my paintings, but I could tell my style was not everyone's cup of tea. By the end of the night, I had sold the hummingbird painting, and all the cards with my contact information were taken. When the last person left, Beth, Celeste, and I decompressed with a glass of wine.

"Ladies, congratulations on a very successful event." Beth raised her glass, and we both joined her. "Celeste, the guests just loved your food, and everyone raved about the service you and your team provided. Thank you."

"We enjoyed every minute. Thank you for the opportunity," Celeste replied.

"And Evie, you sold a painting. Not bad for your first showing."

"Well, thank you for introducing me to Eloise. She is such a wonderful woman. Her energy definitely matches that of the painting. It has found a perfect home."

Beth nodded in agreement.

"Beth, I wanted to echo what Celeste said about you providing the opportunity. Both Celeste and I have taken some big leaps of faith, and you were given to us to help springboard our new lives. I so appreciate you and your generosity. Thank you."

Beth smiled. "Just paying it forward. When I first came to this island, it was scary, and I didn't know if I could make it on my own. Newly divorced, trying to raise my kids and wanting to live my dream of being an artist. There were people who stepped up for me and helped me along the way. I always said that I would do the same and, *ta da!* you two show up. I believe in raising all ships."

We drank to that.

Later, we said our goodnights, and I packed up my car.

Just as I was about to drive out, Steve came to the car window.

"Hey, congratulations."

"Oh, you scared me. Thank you. Hey, you were a big part of this. If you hadn't introduced me to Beth, I wouldn't be here now."

He smiled. "I know talent when I see it."

There was an awkward silence. I could tell we both wanted to address the elephant in the room, but neither one of us did.

"Oh, Steve, I committed to teaching at the high school. Thanks for pushing me."

"Like I said, I know talent when I see it. Those kids will really benefit from your something-something way of painting."

We both laughed.

"Well, thanks again. Have a great night."

Driving home, I thought about Steve. I hadn't thought of him in any way other than a friend. I wondered why Eloise would think we were more.

***

Where was that Zoom link? I swear, I leave corporate America, and now I can't find anything in my email.

I rushed over to the mirror to check my makeup, hair, and dress before I logged on. Then I sat on the couch and propped the computer up on a few books to create the best angle. *Okay, here we go.* I clicked on the link and entered the waiting room. I could hear Hendrix and Aja talking, but I couldn't see them.

"Okay, ready, honey?"

"Uh-huh."

Then their wonderful faces appeared on the screen.

"Hey, Evie."

"Hi, Hendrix."

Hendrix looked at Aja and said, "Aja, I would like you to meet—"

"Evie!" Aja shouted with a beautiful smile. "You paint pretty pictures."

My eyes welled up immediately. She was beautiful in her holiday dress. Her smile warmed me to my core.

"Aja, it is so nice to meet you. How are you feeling?"

"I am perfect. Daddy tells me so."

"Yes, you are, my angel. You are perfect," Hendrix replied.

"Aja, are you excited about Christmas?"

"Yes. I get two. One with Daddy and one with Mommy."

"Wow, you are a lucky little girl with so many people who love you."

"You are lucky, too."

"Huh? What do you mean?" I asked.

"You are lucky because Daddy loves you, too. He told me so."

"Oh, he did, did he?"

"And he says that one day—"

"Okay, baby boo, that's enough," Hendrix interrupted. "Let's not tell all of Daddy's secrets.

"Did you get our package?" he asked me.

"Yes, I have it right here."

"Good. Aja wanted to see you open her holiday gift."

"Yes, open it, open it!" Aja chimed in.

"Okay. Here we go." I cut the tape then opened the box. Inside was a beautifully wrapped package.

"Don't go trying to save the bow. You are driving us crazy over here," Hendrix warned.

I opened the first package. It was a framed photo of Hendrix and Aja.

"Oh, my goodness, you two are adorable."

"You put that next to your bed so you will see us when you first wake up. That is where I have Daddy's picture at Mommy's house," Aja explained.

"Thank you. I can't think of a better way to start my day than to see your smiling faces."

"'Kay. Open mine!" Aja cheered.

When I unwrapped the second gift, I had to hold back the tears. "Aja, did you paint this?"

"Yes, I painted it when I got out of the hospital."

"It is amazing. Can you tell me about it?"

"Daddy told me that painting helps you with your feelings."

"Yes, it does."

"I was sad to be in the hospital, but then you gave me a big Teddy bear, and I was happy."

"I love it, and I will proudly hang it in my house for all to see. Thank you for such a thoughtful gift."

"You're welcome."

"Okay, honey. Let Daddy talk with Evie now."

"Good night, Evie."

"Good night, Aja. Sweet dreams."

"So, you liked your gifts?" Hendrix probed.

"They are wonderful. Just meeting Aja was enough, but then you tugged the heartstrings even more with your photo and her painting. Do you know how hard it was for me not to just turn into a puddle?"

"I'm so glad that you liked the gifts. Thank you for spending your night with us. And, by the way, you look amazing. Wish I was there to see that dress in person."

"Soon, I hope, very soon."

***

Christmas Eve, Granddad and I had gone over to the Townhall to join everyone for the annual potluck. It had been a great turnout, and Santa had come on the firetruck to give presents to all the children.

Morning came, and I made a special breakfast of eggs benedict and fried potatoes for Granddad. After we finished, I gave him my present.

"Kid, you didn't have to give me a present. I have all that I need right here."

"Well, you don't have this." I presented him with the painting that I had done after I had learned about my father.

"Oh, Evie, this is amazing."

I gave Granddad the backstory, and I could tell it filled him with emotion.

"He is so proud of you, kid. I can feel him all around us now. Thank you." Then he slid a small tissue paper wrapped gift over to me. "Hope you like it."

I unwrapped a stunning wampum bracelet.

"I figured you needed an adult-sized one."

"Granddad, you made this?"

"I'm not just an old fisherman. I have been known to do other things."

"You are an artist. Thank you. I love it."

CHAPTER 13 — HEY TEACH

The halls felt so small, but the sounds, lockers, and smells were all the same. Walking into the art room was exhilarating for me. The easels, metal chairs, paint spattered walls, it was the perfect playground to expand the mind and release the spirit.

The bell rang, and students rushed into the room. I was instantaneously thrown back to junior year of high school—backpacks, gossiping, kids jostling and teasing each other. Before I addressed the class, I closed my eyes and asked the Universe for strength and guidance.

"Hello. My name is Evie Prince, and I will be your painting instructor for this session," I interrupted the chatter and could feel all eyes on me. "Okay, to start, how many of you have painted before?" I looked around the room at the few hands raised. "Great. Well, I hope I can provide the people who have painted before with some new techniques. And, for those of you who have never painted, my hope is that you will discover a new world of creativity.

"Let's go around the class so you can tell me your names. This is for my own notes. If you feel you need to make up a name, please make it good and know I will call you that for the entire session. However, I'll know you're goofing me since I have the class roster right here." I held up a sheet of paper.

The kids went around the room, and most of them gave me their real names. There was always one, but in this class, there were two who needed to stand out. One girl, Sophie, wanted to be called Bubba, and another boy, Jake, asked to be called Rufus. By the time we got through the names and giggles, we only had fifteen minutes left in class, so I provided them a brief lesson on the differences between oil paints versus water paints and why I preferred to work in oil.

Just as the class was about to break, the door opened and a young man entered.

"Hi. Can I help you?"

"Uh, yeah. I'm Josh, and I just got placed in this class."

I looked at the roster and checked off his name.

"Hi, Josh. Welcome. Have you painted before?"

"Uh, no, never." He looked around the room nervously.

"Great. You are in good company. Neither have I," I replied with a grin.

Before Josh could sit down, the bell rang, and the class dispersed quicker than I could say dismissed. Josh wasn't so quick to leave. He was looking at his schedule, trying to figure out his next class. I could tell he wasn't from the island.

"Did you just move to the island?"

"Yeah," he responded. "How did you know?"

"I could just tell. You from out West?"

"Yeah, California."

"Well, welcome to the island."

Josh looked up from his class schedule with a surprised look, like no one had said that to him before. Then he smiled and said, "Thanks."

On my way out of the school, I popped my head into the teachers' lounge to see if Mr. Frank was around.

"Hiya. How was your first class?" Mr. Frank asked, his voice filled with curiosity.

"Short. By the time I got them settled and we did introductions, I only had a little time to do my lesson."

"I wouldn't worry too much about that. You can jump right into it for your next class."

"Any words of wisdom?"

He laughed. "Just be yourself. They are human, just like you. If you make a mistake, oh well. They prefer when a teacher is real. I wouldn't try to be their friend or act their age. That ship has sailed." He chuckled.

"Ha-ha. Yes, it sailed a long time ago. Thanks for the reminder," I teased with a disapproving look.

***

I taught two days a week. So, by the second week, we got into the groove. The class seemed to enjoy each other. There was plenty of banter, so the energy in the room was high, but we still got work done. Those who had painted before really had skill, and this was just an outlet for them to have more creative time. For those who hadn't painted before, there was trepidation to open themselves up.

"Okay, okay, everyone settle down, please. I want to start today's class with a slideshow. I've noticed that there is concern by many to open yourselves up to paint freely. Please understand that I am not grading your paintings. Your exam will be on the techniques that I teach you. So, after today's slideshow, I hope you will all feel comfortable just being yourself and enjoying the painting process."

I started the slideshow with my early paintings and asked for the class to critique them.

"Thank you for being so polite, but what I take away from your comments is that they are just okay. Now, let me show you how I currently paint."

There was a murmur in the room.

"Okay, so what do you think? Bubba, how does this painting make you feel?"

The class giggled, hearing me call Sophie *Bubba*.

"It is different."

"In what way?" I asked.

"Your first paintings were nice, but this one is edgy."

"Would you classify it as ugly?"

"Well … it's dark."

"Exactly! That is exactly how I was feeling. I entitled this painting "Me," because I was going through a lot or emotional stuff."

I looked over to see Josh raise his hand. "Yes, Josh."

"I can see struggle, but there is also clarity."

"Nice. You are correct. When I painted this piece, it helped me work through my feelings. That is how I paint all of my work. I paint my feelings. This is what I call the something-something technique."

"The something-something technique?" Rufus asked sarcastically.

"Yup, made it up myself," I responded. "Let me ask you this. When you sit quietly, do you ever hear a voice in your head?"

The kids all looked at each other like I was crazy.

"Yes, you may all think that I'm crazy, which I could be, but if you allow yourself to listen, you will hear a voice. I call it my higher self. Some people call it God. Others, Source."

"I didn't know this was theology class?" Anne yelled out from the back.

"It's not. Just hear me out. Before our next class, I would like all of you to find some quiet time and listen. You will hear things. Some may be positive, some negative, but you will hear. I don't want to know what you heard, but I would like you to paint the emotion that you felt when you heard it."

The room got quiet.

I went through the rest of the slideshow to reinforce the difference between when I was just seeing and painting to when I was feeling and painting.

The bell rang, and everyone bolted from the room. Josh lingered.

"What's up?" I probed.

"Uh …" He paused. "I just wanted to say that I understood what you meant about hearing a voice."

"Does it scare you?"

"A little. What I hear is bad."

"What do you mean, *bad*?"

"Never mind. I gotta get to my next class." Josh grabbed his bag and walked out.

Per usual, I stopped by the teachers' lounge to chat with Mr. Frank about how things were going.

"So, Teach, how did it go?"

"Today was a great day," I announced. "I introduced my something-something technique."

"Well, that sounds really technical," Mr. Frank joked.

"It's simply painting your feelings or emotions versus just painting what you see."

"Hmm … What did they think?"

"I was crazy. But it seemed to resonate with one student. What is Josh's backstory?"

"Funny you should ask. His story is similar to yours—moved here to live with his grandparents after his mother died."

"Oh, it seems like he is looking for some help or friendship."

"Well, you would be the perfect one to help him."

"I don't want to interfere."

"Wonder if I didn't interfere."

"Good point."

***

The following week at class, I asked everyone to jump right in and start painting. I had positioned the easels in a circle so that no one could see each other's work. It took some time but, by halfway through the class, everyone had paint on their canvas. The bell rang and, unlike other days when everyone bolted, it seemed like they didn't want to leave.

"Okay, everyone. Do we need more time to finish these paintings?"

A few students said *yes*, Josh being one of them.

"All right, I'll be here tomorrow for two hours, twelve to two. If your schedule allows, you can stop by and finish up your pieces. If that doesn't work for you, email me and we can hopefully find some more time."

***

I hadn't seen Granddad in a few days, so I offered to make us dinner. I made a nice Crock Pot of shredded beef with homemade tortillas and all the fixings.

"Hey, kid, this is superb. Nice to have something different."

"Glad you like it. Can I ask you something?"

"Sure. What is it?"

"When I first lost my mother, how did you reach me?"

"What do you mean, *reach you*?"

"Well, I know I had to have been closed off, but somehow, you always got me to share my feelings."

"Why do you ask?"

"I have a student who may be in the same boat. Just moved here from California to live with his grandparents after his mother died."

"Oh. Well, I gave you your space and just planted seeds. I tried to relate to you as best as I could by letting you know that other people have similar feelings. You were confused, and I tried to let you know it was okay."

"You did a good job. I didn't know it then, but you really kept me grounded and feeling like I wasn't alone."

"We are never alone."

***

I arrived at the school at eleven thirty so I could get set up and take some time looking at everyone's paintings. Right at noon, I heard a knock on the door. It was Josh.

"Come on in."

"Hi, Ms. Prince."

"I have your paints set up right over there."

"Thanks." Josh went over to grab his paints and set himself up.

"Josh, did I ever tell you I lived out West—well, more middle—but many consider it out West. I moved out here from Colorado. Moved into my grandparents' house …"

"Oh."

"Yup. I moved to the island after my mother died, and I came to live with my grandparents. Went to this high school for a couple of years."

I could see Josh looking at me from over his canvas.

"It was rough, but Mr. Frank—Hey, do you have Mr. Frank for Trig?"

"No, I have Mrs. Bennett."

"Oh, I had Mr. Frank. Anyway, he was always nice to me. Made my time here pretty nice. If you have time to meet him, I would. He's a great guy."

We didn't talk much more after that since more students arrived, but I planted the seed.

Next class, I had all the paintings arranged like they were in a gallery. No one knew whose was who. I asked the students to write about their feelings or the emotions that they felt after looking at each painting. Once everyone had finished, I arranged the comments next to each painting and wrapped them up so that they could take them home.

"Before everyone leaves, stop by my desk, and I will give you back your paintings. They will be wrapped, and I will include your classmates' comments. Next class, I would like to see if the emotion that you felt painting your pieces was the same emotion that your classmates felt looking at your pieces." I looked around the room. "Does anyone want to share how they felt after this exercise?"

"It was kind of cool," Rufus shared.

"Yeah, I could get some stuff off my chest," another student admitted.

"Good. That was my hope. As my grandmother told me, the more emotions you feel when you paint, the more it will be expressed in your painting."

The bell rang, and everyone filed up to my desk to pick up their pieces. When I got to Josh, he said, "Thank you," but I could tell it wasn't for the painting.

Before I could get to the teachers' lounge, Mr. Frank was at my classroom door.

"Guess who said hello to me today?"

"Who?"

"Josh."

"Oh, good. I told him you were a nice guy, and that you helped me when I came to the high school."

"Gee, thanks. I appreciate that."

"I wanted to make sure that he had someone to go to, since I'm just a flash in the pan."

"I wouldn't say that. There has been a buzz about you. I heard what your students have been saying. They enjoy your class. Mind you, they won't tell you, but I heard it myself."

I blushed. "Thank you. This has been a real eye-opener. It feels good to share my love of painting with others."

***

The following week's class was an emotional eye-opener for many of the students.

"So, how do you feel about the comments your classmates made about your paintings? Were they correct?"

No one responded.

"Hmm … No one has anything to say?"

Josh raised his hand. "They were right."

"Wonderful. Your emotions were felt by the viewer. That is what every artist hopes for, that what they are trying to portray is felt or it creates emotions in the person experiencing the painting. Anyone else?"

"Mostly, they got what I was trying to say," Bubba added.

"Good. Well, I hope this illustrates my earlier point. The more emotion you put into your painting, the more the viewer will feel."

Since there was little discussion, I gave a brief lecture on composition. Per usual, when the bell rang, the class was out the door immediately. Josh, however, lingered.

"Josh, thanks for your comments. The class was a little quiet today."

"Ms. Prince, can I ask you something?"

"Sure. What is it?"

He paused. "Please don't think that I'm weird."

"Of course not."

"Well, I hear voices all the time. Ever since my mother died, it seems like I can't not hear them. Did you hear voices when your mother died?"

"I didn't know it then, but yes, I did. There was a lot of internal struggle. I wasn't told how my mother died. After I learned of her death, my grandparents acted like nothing had happened. I was confused and felt like I had no one to talk with."

"I wish that were my case. My grandparents can't stop talking about my mother and how they miss her."

"Can you understand why they say that?"

"Yes, but it makes me feel guilty."

"Why?"

Josh lowered his head. "Because I couldn't save her."

"I don't mean to pry, but can you tell me how she died?"

"It was a car accident. My mom was driving, and someone ran a red light and hit her directly. Once I came to, I couldn't get her out of the car. They pulled me away before the car exploded."

"Oh, Josh, I am sorry. That is a lot of emotion to be carrying around."

"I don't want to go home after school because my grandparents cry a lot. She was their only child."

"They are in pain, just like you are, but you are all dealing with it in different ways. Is painting helping you?"

"Yes, I can get out my frustration and anger."

"That is wonderful. Do you have the ability to paint at home?"

"Not really."

"Okay, let me think about this and see if there is something that I can do."

Josh just looked at me.

"Before you go, let me just say this. Try to look at your grandparents through the eyes of love."

"What do you mean?"

"Try to put yourself in their place. It may be hard, but if you can understand where they are coming from, it replaces the frustration and anger with love. Believe you me, I know it is hard. I have been doing this since I moved to the island, and I continue to do it. But I have learned a lot about my grandparents and me in the process. Tonight, instead of just going to your room after school, why don't you ask your grandparents if they could tell you about your mom as a child. There will be tears, but it will also bring up happy memories. And you will learn things about your mother that you would never have known.

"Josh, this is going to be a journey, but it's better that you deal with it now than, like me, wait till you get older. Emotional pain can stay quiet for a long time, and when you least expect it, it will smack you upside the head and turn your world upside down."

***

I poked my head into the teachers' lounge. "Mr. Frank, can you talk? Outside?"

"Sure, Evie. What's up? Didn't think I would see you today."

We walked out into the courtyard, and I gave him a recap of my conversation with Josh.

"Wow, that's a lot of emotional baggage for a kid to have."

"Yes, I know. He said that painting is helping him release his frustration and anger. I know Josh's situation is different from other kids, but I can see that many kids are dealing with emotions that they just don't know what to do with. I was thinking …"

"That you could teach more kids how to paint and to find a productive way to release their anger?"

"You read my mind."

"Great minds think alike," he said with a smile. "Let me get with the guidance counselor and some others and see what we can do."

"That would be wonderful."

"You understand that if I can pull this off, you are in for the long haul."

I closed my eyes and took a deep breath. "Yes, it's time to pay if forward."

CHAPTER 14 — I GOT YOUR BACK

In the distance, I could hear my phone ringing. Where did I put that thing? I looked through the entire house. It was like playing that kids' game, Marco Polo. With each ring, I was getting hotter or colder. I finally found my phone in my closet, on a shelf, and answered just before it went to voice mail.

"Hello?" I answered in a harried voice.

"Evie, it's Brian."

"Hey, Brian. How are you? Are you treating my girl like the queen she is?"

"Well, that's why I'm calling."

"What? What's wrong? Is Reva okay?" I pummeled him with questions.

"Yes, Reva is fine and healthy, but …"

"But what?"

"It's the wedding. She is avoiding planning the wedding."

"Why would you think that?"

"Because every time we talk about it, she gets quiet and distant. I thought women got excited to plan a wedding."

I took a deep, calming breath before I respond.

"Evie, you still there?"

"First, please do not lump all women together. Not every woman believes in the fairy tale wedding with a big, white dress."

"Oh."

"I will not get on my soapbox, because I can tell you are truly concerned, but that thinking comes across as chauvinistic. Every woman is different and not all want to be a princess and swept off her feet. There are many of us who would rather find a partner who they can spend their life with, and guess what? Reva is one of them." I paused to let my words sink in. "Let me ask you: what kind of a wedding do you want to have?"

"I don't care, but I thought that women always wanted a big wedding with bridesmaids, etcetera."

I cringed. "Again, why do you think Reva is like *all women*? I don't want to be rude, but for the longevity of your relationship, you better understand who you are marrying. She is different, and you need to understand and appreciate that fact."

"I know she's different. That's makes her so attractive to me," he explained.

"Have you asked her what type of wedding she wants?"

"No."

"Hmm … Well, I would start there. I know what she wants, and I know her concerns, but it's not up to me to tell you. You need to find out what they are. You need to ask the questions. It will tell you a lot about her."

Brian was quiet for a moment. "You're right. I just got caught up in all the noise from my family."

"Last question, Brian. Whose wedding is this?"

"What do you mean? It's Reva and mine, of course."

"Just remember that. Good luck and know that I am here if you need me."

"Thanks?" Brian said with trepidation.

***

For the past few nights, Josh had been on my mind. Did I give him the right advice? When I meditated on this question, nothing came to me. I couldn't hear anything clearly. I needed assistance, so I reached out to Colbie for help.

"Colbie, do you have time for a friend question?"

While I waited for her to answer and to keep myself from stewing on the issue, I tried to clean the house. Finally, she called me.

"Hey, Evie. What's up?"

I gave her the rundown on Josh, my advice to him, and that I couldn't get an answer to my question. She was quiet for a few minutes.

"Well, you're not getting an answer because there is no answer. There is no right or wrong."

"*Ugh*, I know that, but …"

"But, what?"

"I just wanted to know that I gave him good advice."

"Was the advice from your heart?"

"Yes, it was."

"Then it was good advice. Why are you so concerned?"

"I just don't want Josh to have to go through what I went through—questioning himself."

"Evie, you realize that is your ego talking, right?"

"What do you mean?"

"Only ego puts labels on things, like right and wrong, good or bad. Josh is on his own journey. You cannot change his path. Only he can. You may have given him the best advice in the world, but that doesn't mean he will follow it, or if he does, if he will take anything away from the conversations that he has with his grandparents. All you can do is hold space for him, send him healing energy, and let him know you are there for him with no judgment."

"Okay, okay, I hear ya. Thank you. I remember you telling me when I first started this journey that ego does not play fair. Yet another example."

"It happens to everyone. I always ask myself: if the belief is limiting, then it is ego. Try not to judge. What you gave was guidance, plain and simple.

"Hey, on another note, how are things going back there? I don't see you on the schedule, so it seems like you have made peace with your feelings toward your grandparents."

"The more questions I ask, the more information I receive. I try to look at all of it with loving eyes. That's all that I can do."

"Good. That is excellent. Take it day by day, check your chakras, protect yourself, never stop asking questions, appreciate, and give yourself grace. That is a good formula for happiness."

"Thank you, Colbie. Thank you for everything."

"You're welcome. Talk again soon."

***

My time as a teacher at the high school was ending, and the students were getting ready for their final exams. It had been a wonderful semester getting to know each one of them. Hanging around the young ones helped me look at the world differently.

The last day of class was open to answer any questions they had about the exam. I also gave each student a Bob Ross painting book to keep them inspired and painting fluffy clouds. Only a few students who painted before had gotten the humor in my gift.

When the bell rang, I said my goodbyes, wishing each one inspiration and the strength to paint freely and without judgment. Josh was the last student. He seemed to hang around, so I knew he wanted to talk with me.

"Ms. Prince, can I tell you something?"

"Sure. What's up?"

"Please don't think I'm weird, but I don't have anyone else I can tell this to."

"Don't worry; no judgment here."

Josh stammered for a moment then finally said, "My mom visited me in my dreams last night."

"Wow, that is wonderful. How do you feel?"

"Actually, really good. She said that there was nothing that I could have done to save her and to be gentle with my grandparents." His eyes misted.

"That is very special, Josh. To have that spiritual connection with your mother is just the beginning to so much more."

"What do you mean?"

"When people die, it is only their physical presence that leaves us. Their soul, or spirit, stays with us always. Many people are too closed down to understand. But when you allow yourself to be open, the most miraculous things happen. I speak with my grandparents regularly. This, however, is only recent since I was closed down to them for several reasons. Having them back in my life is pure joy."

Josh gave me an earnest look.

"Your mother is with you *always*. All you have to do is speak with her. She will respond. Maybe not in the way you think, so keep your eyes and ears open."

"Thanks, Ms. Prince."

"You're welcome."

"Um … I know you are leaving after this semester, but can I talk with you if I need to?"

"Of course. You have my email. Reach out any time."

Right before Josh walked out the door, he turned and gave me a smile.

***

As usual, I visited the teachers' lounge before heading out. When I poked my head in, though, I didn't see Mr. Frank anywhere. I asked the other teachers, and they said that he had fallen ill and would not be in for the rest of the week.

On the drive back up island, I had a knot in my stomach. Something didn't feel right. This feeling was nagging at me.

I pulled over to quiet my mind and figure out what was going on. As soon as I did, I heard distinctively, *"Go to the hospital."*

I turned the car around and headed directly to the hospital. When I walked into the front lobby, I saw Steve speaking with a few other people.

"Evie, what are you doing here?"

"I-I was guided to come to the hospital, but I don't know why. Why are you here?"

"Bill is in the hospital."

"Bill?"

"Bill Frank."

"What? I knew there was something wrong when I didn't see him in the teachers' lounge this afternoon. What happened?"

"They don't know. He said he's been feeling off for the past couple of weeks. Just couldn't shake it. He's in now for testing," Steve explained.

"So, what is your connection to Mr. Frank?"

"Oh, we met when I was going through rehab. He also served as a mentor to me. People like us try to stick together. The network is tight."

"I didn't know. Please let him know I stopped by."

"I will."

***

It had been an emotional day, and all I wanted to do after dinner was crawl into bed and talk with Hendrix.

"Good evening."

"Good evening, beautiful. You sound tired."

"I am. It was a long day. Last day of actual class, and Mr. Frank was admitted into the hospital."

"Oh no. Why?"

"They don't know yet. Steve has a connection to him and said he would keep me posted."

"Wow, that is a long day. I have something that may cheer you up. Just a second." There were muffled sounds on the other end. Then I heard this sweet voice.

"Hi, Evie."

"Hi, Aja. How are you?"

"I'm good. Daddy and I are having a sleepover."

"Wow, that sounds like a lot of fun."

"It is And, if I'm a good girl, I can have ice cream for dessert."

"What kind?"

"Daddy, what kind of ice cream?" Aja yells, not completely moving the phone away from her mouth.

"Mint chocolate chip," Hendrix yells back.

"Mint chocolate chip," Aja replies.

"Mmm … That sounds so good."

"Do you want me to save you some?"

"No, but thank you for offering." I giggled.

Hendrix took the phone back.

"OMG, she is so sweet," I gushed.

"Amazing, isn't it? She is made of pure joy. I love feeling her energy."

"Thank you for letting me experience her energy, as well. It made my night."

"I better let you go; you sound exhausted."

I yawned and replied, "Yes, I am. Have a great sleepover."

"We will. I love you, Evie Prince."

"I love you, Hendrix Talisman."

***

After an amazing night's sleep, I woke refreshed and ready for whatever came my way. Or, so I thought.

I looked at my phone and saw a message from Steve.

"Evie, it's Steve. I was just notified by the hospital that Bill went into cardiac arrest last night. Call me!"

What? How could this happen?

I dialed Steve's number immediately.

"What's going on?" was the first question I hit Steve with before he could say hello.

"Things are unclear. He doesn't have any family, so I'm only given so much information."

"How is he doing now?"

"It doesn't sound good."

"Can we see him?"

"We can try."

"Okay, I'll pick you up on the way."

The drive over to the hospital was tense. Neither one of us knew what to expect when we got there. When we walked into the hospital, I saw the intern who had helped Granddad.

"Excuse me."

"Yes?"

"Hi, I don't know if you remember me, but I am Attaquin Brown's granddaughter. We met when—"

"Oh yeah, I remember. Attaquin isn't back here, is he?"

"No, no, he's not. But we have a good friend who is in here. Bill Frank."

"Ah, yes."

"Can you tell us how he's doing?" I knew he could see the concern on both our faces.

"Well, I can't tell you much, but he isn't doing very well."

"Is there a chance we can see him?" Steve interjected.

"Um … Hold on. Let me check something." The intern went to the desk and talked to the nurses on duty. When he returned, he said, "You have five minutes. No more." Then he walked us to Mr. Frank's room.

The room was dimly lit. Most of the light was coming from all the monitors they had hooked him up to. Steve was almost in shock. I grabbed him by the arm and led him over to the bed, placing Mr. Frank's left hand into Steve's. Then I moved to the other side of the bed and took his other hand. There was no response from Mr. Frank.

Looking at Steve, I said, "Think of any memory of Mr. Frank that brings you joy." When he had that memory, I then instructed, "Send that feeling of joy and love through his hand." And I did the same. Memories of me walking into the teachers' lounge and him calling me Teach. The smile he would always give me. Looking back, that smile had always been filled with pride. Tears of joy and sadness streamed down my face.

When I opened my eyes, I looked at Steve. His head was hung low, and he was trying to wipe the tears from his face, but it was no use.

As I started to let go of Mr. Frank's hand, I felt the faintest squeeze, and then I heard the monitor alarm go off. He was leaving us.

Doctors and nurses ran into the room and ushered us to the back of the room. They tried to revive him, but he was gone.

I looked at Steve, and he was just sobbing. We hugged and wept together.

***

The drive back up island was quiet. When we got to Steve's house, he put his hand on the door handle then looked back at me. "Evie, why did you have us hold his hands?"

"I knew he would not be with us much longer. I wanted him to know that we were there with him and that we were sending him love. It was as much for us as for him. I wanted him to know that, when he left his physical life for the spiritual, that he was not alone."

Steve closed his eyes, trying to hold back the tears. "I could have sworn, before he passed, I felt him squeeze my hand. I can't tell if it really happened, or if I wanted it so badly that I thought it happened."

"It happened, because I felt it, as well. He was letting us know that he felt us, and it was time for him to move on."

***

Mourners filled the entire high school auditorium. Every walk of life was there—current and former students, colleagues, community members. Mr. Frank had said that he didn't have family but, in reality, living on an island, the community became your family.

Granddad attended the memorial with me. We saw Steve, Beth, and several other people who we knew as we walked in.

The high school principal served as the celebrant for the memorial service. He asked that anyone who wished to say something in honor of Mr. Frank to come to the podium. Each story shared highlighted how much of a pillar he had been in the community. There was not a dry eye in the place. To my surprise, Steve stood to make a comment.

"Bill Frank, like many others of us in this audience, struggled with life at times. He turned to alcohol and tried to bury his demons. He suffered, but after a lot of focus, he came out a better man. That man served as one of my mentors when I was in a similar place in life. He was tough on me, but it was because he loved me and didn't want me to continue to live in the dark.

"Bill grew up on the island. He loved this place. Every time he tried to leave, he would look at the ocean and decide to stay another year. When his parents passed many years ago, he said that he didn't have any family left. But I don't agree. Look around this room. This was Bill's family. He affected each one of us. Everyone has a story about Bill Frank. He made this island a better place, and I hope to become half the man he was." When Steve returned to his seat, he looked over at me, and I gave him a smile.

***

A few weeks passed, and I came home to an envelope at the door. *"Evie Prince"* was written on the outside, but I didn't recognize the handwriting. Opening the envelope, I found it was filled with pictures and newspaper articles about me. The last thing in the envelope was a picture of Mr. Frank and my dad, both with enormous smiles on their faces. My dad's arm was around his shoulders. "*I got your back. ALWAYS!*" was written on the back of the photo.

I took the photo and slipped it into the hallway mirror. To see their faces and to feel their energy was something that I wanted to feel every day.

CHAPTER 15 — JACK OF ALL TRADES

"*Hey, I need to talk with you. Please call me.*"

"What's up?" I asked when I called Reva.

"Hey, girl. Thanks for calling."

"Is everything okay?"

"Yes. All is good. I just wanted to talk with you about the wedding."

My heart sank. I hoped Brian hadn't fallen back into his old ways. "Sure."

"Remember the discussion we had when you came out to visit about who is the wedding for?"

"Yes."

"Well, Brian and I have been talking, and he shut down all the noise from his family about having a big wedding."

"He did, did he?"

"Why did you say it like that? Evie, did you say something to Brian?"

"No way. I wouldn't do that." I wasn't a good poker player, so I hoped she couldn't tell I was lying.

"Anyway, we have decided to have a very intimate wedding, and then have a larger family gathering later."

"That sounds like a brilliant plan."

"So, what are you doing this weekend?"

"Huh?"

"We decided to get married at the same spot as he proposed on the island. All we need is a Justice of the Peace and a witness. Will you be our witness?"

"Of course I'll be your witness! Reva, I am so happy for you. Brian is cool with this?"

"Yes, he didn't care about the wedding. All he wanted was to get married. He thought I wanted all the big, white wedding stuff. So, can you ask the owner of the studio if we could use her front yard? I've already arranged for the Justice of the Peace."

"Definitely."

As soon as I got off the phone with Reva, I called Beth.

"Beth, this is Evie. Have a huge favor to ask."

"Sure. What's up?"

"Do you remember my friend who got engaged at your studio?"

"Of course. That was a wonderful surprise."

"Well, they would like to get married in the same spot. Can we borrow your front yard?"

***

There was still a lot to do, even though Reva and Brian were getting married by the Justice of the Peace. I spoke with Brian and asked if I could arrange for an amazing dinner after the wedding as my gift to them. He agreed. Reva wouldn't have any idea what I was up to.

That evening, when Hendrix and I spoke, I gave him the wonderful news.

"This weekend?"

"Yes. Amazing, isn't it?"

"Who's your date?" he asked hesitantly.

"No date. It's just the happy couple, the Justice of the Peace, and me, the witness." I could feel Hendrix's relief. "I'm going to surprise them by arranging for a special dinner after the ceremony."

"That sound very romantic."

"Anything for my girl."

"Well, I look forward to the day when I get to meet her."

"Yes, it will be soon, I promise."

***

The day was finally here. They had a car waiting for them when they got off the boat that took them directly to their bed and breakfast. The Justice of the Peace, photographer, and I arrived at the studio about an hour before sunset. Beth and I arranged everything, and now all we had to do was wait for the happy couple.

About fifteen minutes before sunset, their car arrived. Reva was just beaming, dressed in a beautiful but simple ivory dress that highlighted all that her momma gave her. Brian was in a dapper blue suit. The weather was still on the cool side, so Reva had a stunning ivory and blue wrap. It was all I could do to stop myself from crying. I was so happy for them.

The ceremony was brief but beautiful. Reva and Brian had written their own vows. Both were heartfelt and just dripping with love.

Right as the colors in the sky reached their peak, they were pronounced husband and wife. Brian took Reva in his arms and, with a flourish, bent her slightly backward and gave her an intoxicatingly sensual kiss. We all blushed a little, feeling like we were intruding.

When all was said and done, the photographer took several photos, and then Brian popped a bottle of champagne.

"Let's raise our glasses to the happy couple. Congratulations, Reva and Brian! May you feel this love every day," I toasted.

We clinked glasses.

"Reva and Brian, as my gift to you, please join me in the studio," I ceremonially requested.

The studio was lit with those wonderful twinkly lights. The room was warm, and the atmosphere was sexy but cozy. In the middle was a table with a white tablecloth set for two. The tableware was gold-accented and sparkled in the lights. Soft jazz played in the background.

Reva and Brian were seated, and then Celeste catered an amazing dinner. She had prepared the most decadent food. She was truly talented.

The rest of us enjoyed our own meal in Beth's house. Only Celeste and the photographer interacted with the couple. They were in their own little world.

When it was time for dessert, the rest of us joined the couple. Even Granddad made a brief appearance to give his congratulations. The champagne flowed as we all laughed, danced, and enjoyed the magic in the room.

"Evie, how did you pull this all off?"

"What do you mean?"

"Seriously, Evie, dinner was wonderful. You outdid yourself," Brian complimented.

"I know people," was all I said.

"I know your car is waiting to take you back, but I have one more thing that I wanted to give you." In the room's corner was an easel covered in a white cloth. "This is to remind you of the magic of the night you committed yourselves to each other." I removed the cloth, and Reva gasped, jumped up, and then gave me an enormous hug.

"Evie, this is magnificent. Thank you." Brian joined the embrace.

I turned to Brian. "Welcome to the family."

***

The next morning, I met the two love birds for lunch before they headed back on the boat.

"I wish you could stay longer," I whined.

"This summer, we will schedule a proper vacation," Reva promised.

Brian nodded in agreement.

My eyes misted as we said our goodbyes. Then I yelled out as they got on the boat, "I love you, Reva."

She turned with a smile. "I love ya, girl."

***

Slowly, the weather started warming up and, in no time, summer would be here again. The winter wasn't as bad as I they had claimed. The quiet had let me paint and create a small inventory of my work. I hadn't shared it all with Tatum, but I needed to decide what I wanted to do. The website that I was supposed to have built months ago still only provided my contact information. The business side of art didn't interest me as much as the actual painting. Still, it was something that I needed to get better at.

I reached out to Beth to ask for some guidance.

"Hello. This is Beth."

"Hi, Beth. It's Evie."

"Hey, Evie. How are you doing?"

"Great. Hey, I wanted to see if I could pick your brain over lunch one day. Still trying to get my business side together."

"Sure. I have time this week."

"Wonderful. How does Wednesday sound? I will make us lunch here, if that works for you?"

"Yes, that sounds great."

Since I hadn't been selling regularly, the money had been ebbing and flowing. The less that I looked at my bank account, the less stress that I had. The business was still in the red, but after a year, I was feeling good with the direction that I was heading in.

To prepare for my meeting, I pulled out the old marketing plan that Tatum and I had created before leaving Denver—website, social media, gallery showings. Well, I started a website, and I had a showing, so not too bad. I tried to make myself feel better, knowing full well that I needed to focus more on the business.

Thinking about Wednesday's meeting gave me angst. Why was I so wigged-out about this conversation? It needed to be done, yet I was feeling uneasy.

To get some answers, I went outside to meditate. However, my heart was pounding, and I couldn't quiet my mind. *Breathe in, breathe out*, I said to myself. Finally, I counted backward slowly, from ten to one. At last, I was in a quiet mind.

Higher self, why am I so concerned about this discussion with Beth?

"*You are afraid.*"

"Afraid of what?"

"*Success.*"

Hearing that silenced me. I knew immediately this was the truth.

"But, how do I change it?"

"*Bring down your walls. Know it is okay to be vulnerable. Ask for help and believe in yourself.*"

"Geez, is that all?" I asked sarcastically.

"*Your success will only go so far. You have found your passion, but to reach the level you say you desire, you will have to do more.*"

Wow, this was a real eye-opener. I knew many people who had sabotaged their success, but I never thought that I would be one of them.

"Haven't I taken enough leaps of faith?"

"*You are always changing and growing. To reach your fullest potential, let go of old habits and beliefs so new ones can be created.*"

The uneasiness I had about this meeting was nothing compared to the anxiety I was getting, knowing that I had to do more.

***

To make the house look as presentable as possible, I brought out my special chinaware from my old house. The table looked great.

I heard Beth pull into the driveway. She came bearing gifts—an adorable flower arrangement.

"Knock, knock."

"Beth, come on in. Welcome to my humble abode."

"It's a cute place. I didn't realize what an amazing view you have when I was here last."

"Yes, my grandparents really found a perfect spot. Please, sit down."

"Oh, here, I brought these for you."

"Mmm … They smell wonderful. Thank you."

"Everything looks and smells great," Beth complimented. I had made a minestrone soup, fresh bread, sliced cheeses, and meats.

We sat down and jumped right into the food.

In-between bites, Beth asked, "So, you had questions about how I run my business?"

"Yes. So, let me explain what I am currently doing. I have an agent, per se, who helps me sell. We have a great relationship, and she was instrumental in getting me the commissioned work. I would also like to show here at the sunshine studio and maybe do something online. My concern is biting off more than I can chew. I want nothing interfering with me being able to paint."

"Definitely. I understand your concern completely," Beth responded. "My circumstances differed from yours. Since I was a newly single mom with two kids, who just moved to the island, my time needed to be spent in the most expeditious way. I gave myself three months to get settled and to paint as many pieces as possible when my kids were in school. This provided me with inventory. Then I created a website and sold primarily from the site. No one was offering gallery showings, and I did not have the studio yet. You could find me at every artisan fair across the island, peddling my wares. It was a slow go and, after three months, I was working in a deficit. That's where my cousin, Steve, and others stepped in.

"Steve was building homes for some of the richest people on the island. He would leave my business card in unsuspecting places in the new house so the homeowner would stumble upon it, wonder where it came from, and hopefully visit my website. Others talked to gallery owners they knew. I had a makeshift public relations team. I also needed to get out there and talk myself up. This was the hardest part."

"I'm afraid I'll need to do the same," I lamented.

"I'll admit, it felt uncomfortable, but I had to feed my family. I called the local radio station to see if I could be interviewed and did the same with the local papers. Finally, I opened my home and had my first showing. It was at the holiday time, and I knew people were looking for unique gifts, so I splurged and hosted my own show. I don't know if it was one specific thing, or all put together, but I finally started making traction and selling. As things took off, I pulled back from the fairs and was more exclusive. Over the years, I have pulled back even further, and now people can only purchase my work through gallery showings and commissioned work."

"Well, your exclusivity hasn't hurt you."

"No, it hasn't. Actually, I believe it has helped me. I can ask for a higher price for my pieces, and I am being marketed to a different audience."

"This is great information and gives me a lot to think about," I told her.

"Evie, you are already well on your way to having that higher clientele. I have contacts at the galleries that I would be happy to introduce you to. And, when you are ready to have your own show, I can help with the invitation list. People are always looking to discover a new artist, particularly before they get really big and start asking more for their paintings." Beth chuckled. "If I had an agent, I would use her but keep the island for yourself. This is your backyard and your relationships. It is special, and you need to nurturer it. In the end, it will pay off."

"I like that. I like that a lot."

"But you can't forget that you have to put yourself out there. Granted, you don't have to do all the artisan fairs like I did, but people need to see that you are invested and believe in your work. If you don't believe in you, who will?"

"Those are some wise words. I have a very special friend who has also told me the same thing."

"If I had to start somewhere, I would work on the website. That is your calling card. If people can't meet you in person, they can still learn about you through your site."

"I was afraid you were going to say that. I know nothing about updating my website."

"Ask at the high school. I'm sure one of those young whiz kids could help you out."

"Great idea. Thanks."

"Thanks for lunch and the company. I do need to leave so I can get downtown, buy food, and get back before the kids get home from school."

"Of course. Thank you for the time. I really appreciate it."

After Beth left, I grabbed a blanket and headed for the beach. I wanted to open my mind so that I could write about myself.

The sand was damp and cold, but I needed to feel the earth underneath me. The air smelled salty, and a light mist was washing in from the shore.

> *On a journey, guided by the light in her heart*
> *Emotional*
> *Thought provoking*

Leap of faith
Finding herself
Expansion of self and mind.

Words were coming, but how did they fit together? Did people really care about who was painting the piece, or did they just want to feel something from it?

I knew that was ego talking, so I stopped writing and just felt the air on my skin.

Presence of mind. I just wanted to be present. Not worry about anything but what I was feeling in this exact moment.

Then I heard, "*An artist seeking truth of self through her art.*"

Hmm … Not only did that sound pretty good, but it was true.

***

"So, how is married life been treating you?"

"It's crazy how a little ceremony can change everything."

"What do you mean? You guys okay?"

"Hmm … I knew I loved Brian before we got married, but now I feel like the love is deeper, if that's possible."

"Wow, hook, line, and sinker."

"You got that right."

"How did his family take you guys eloping?"

"Once the shock subsided, they understood. We promised that we would have a celebration this summer."

"Nice. So, have you decided where you're going to live?"

"I think it's time to move out of the City."

"Really?"

"Yup. Riding out the pandemic in the City was tough. Not that it wasn't tough in other places, but I would like to be more suburban. Shop in a grocery store versus a bodega. Have a backyard, a little more space."

"So, you're moving to Philly?"

"Actually, we are looking for a new place. Someplace that we can make into *our* home."

"Well, it all sounds lovely, and I am thrilled for you."

"Thanks. If it wasn't for you, I would never have met Brian."

"I don't believe that. If it was meant to be, it would. You would have just met somewhere else. But I am glad that I played a supporting role."

"So, what's up with you and your man?"

"I wouldn't say that he is my man, but I do love him. We are still taking it slow. Now that he is a father, things are more complicated."

"Do they have to be?"

"Huh?"

"Are they more complicated, or are you projecting that they are more complicated?"

"Let's just say there are more people at the table now than before. Not that I'm concerned, but Aja is so young, and she needs both her parents. I don't know if Hendrix will be able to leave her."

"Oh, so there is the assumption that he would move to you?"

Reva's comment was like a bucket of cold water.

"Huh. Yes, I guess I assumed he would, since I had just made this big move and everything."

"What do they say about assuming? *It makes an ass out of you and me.*"

"Okay, okay. When the time comes, if it ever does, that will need to be a topic of discussion."

"It will. Don't worry. Hey, I know this is a random question, but did that other guy ever ask you out?"

"Who?"

"The guy who helped you build the studio."

"Steve? Why would you ask that?"

"Because he asked Brian if you were with anyone."

"What? Why didn't you tell me?"

"I just found out myself. He's cute, and he seems like a nice guy."

"Well, he is, but he's just a friend," I assured.

"Okay, I was just asking. But you will tell me if he does, right?"

"Reva, please, he thinks of me as a friend, as well. Plus, he is younger than me."

"Oh, like that ever stopped you before."

"Hey! Be nice."

Reva giggled. "Gotta go. Love ya."

"Love you, too."

After we hung up, our discussion about Steve lingered with me. It was like she knew something that I didn't.

***

Today was Thursday, so the library was open. I headed over, intending to find a book on website design and to pick up some new movies. When I walked in, Barbra was at the desk.

"Hey, Evie. Long time no see. What have you been up to? Hanging out with those aliens?" She snickered.

"Hi, Barbra. Actually, been doing a lot of painting. But I am hoping you can help me. I need a book on website design. Do you have one?"

Barbra turned to the computer to do a search as I headed over to the movie section.

From behind, I heard, "Why don't you just search on YouTube?"

I turned around to see Steve in the stacks next to me.

My face flushed. "I guess I could do that, as well," I replied.

"So, what is this new project you are working on?"

"Updating my website."

"I could help you with that."

"Seriously? Seems like you are a jack of all trades."

"I have a lot of downtime, so I am always learning something new. What is your site's address? I'll check it out and give you some suggestions."

I looked at him sideways, trying to determine if he was pulling my leg. What could it hurt?

"It's www.eviepaints.com."

"Are you around tomorrow night? I can stop by after work and give you some ideas."

"Yes, I'll be around."

"Great. See you then."

I turned and grabbed a couple of movies off the shelf then headed over to Barbra to check them out.

She looked at me with a sly smile. "So, I guess you don't need me to find you that book, after all."

I gave her a disapproving look. "No, I'm good. Just these movies. Thank you."

On the drive back from the library, thoughts filled my mind. *Can Steve like me? He is cute, but I am in a relationship with Hendrix. Or am I? How does one take things slow? Wonder if Steve asks me out. What do I say?*

I was so lost in thought that I almost hit a mouse in the road. I slammed on my brakes. Luckily, there was no one behind me. Instead of the mouse running away, though, it stood on its hind legs, and I swore it looked me straight in the face. Then it slowly turned and ran into the bushes.

I drove slowly the rest of the way home, but I knew I had just been given a message.

***

"Hey, Granddad. You home?"

"Over here. Cleaning fish."

I walked behind the house, and there he was, knife in hand, gutting his latest catch.

"Looks good," I complimented.

"Yup, blues were running. I was gonna smoke it."

"Mmm … That sounds good. Hey, I grabbed some new movies. Want to come over later, and I'll make some popcorn and we can have a movie night."

"Sounds good. Are you going to kill me with a chick flick, or did you get something that I may find interesting?"

"Don't worry; I wouldn't do that to you. I've been on a sci-fi kick lately."

"Nice. What time?"

"Seven o'clock."

"I'll be there."

***

Just as I was pouring the popcorn into a couple of bowls, Granddad walked in.

"Hey, I brought a couple of beers. Will you join me?"

"Of course. Thanks. The movies are on the table. Pick one and get it started. I'll be right back."

When I returned, Granddad had everything queued up and ready to go.

"Before we start, I believe I received a message today, and I was hoping you could help me out."

"Sure. What happened?"

"On the way home from the library, I almost hit a mouse in the road. When I slammed on my brakes to avoid it, it stood on its hind legs and stared at me. Then it slowly turned and ran away."

"Huh, a mouse. That's very interesting. The mouse sees everything up close and only sees what is in front of it. You are most likely being asked to scrutinize and to pay attention to what is right in front of you."

"That's weird. I wonder what that is about."

Granddad looked at me. "You'll know when it's time to know."

***

At five-thirty, I heard Steve's truck coming up the road. I put my brush down and opened the studio door.

"Hey."

"Hi. Is this a good time?" Steve walked into the studio with a bag in his hand.

"Yup. I just started to clean up. Whatcha got?"

"I didn't know if you'd eaten yet, so I brought some Chinese. Will you join me?"

"Wow, that's nice. Yes, I would love to. I'm almost done here, so you can bring the food into the house."

By the time I finished cleaning and got into the house, Steve had the table set and was waiting for me.

"Wow, thank you."

"No worries."

"Soda?" I asked.

"Please."

Steve served then started eating, asking, "So, what do you want your website to accomplish?"

"Well, it's my business card to the world, really. I would like to tell my prospective buyers about me, sell paintings and other items from it, press, and provide dates for showings."

"Okay, that's not too bad. It's a pretty simple site."

After dinner, we sat at my laptop, and he showed me various examples of sites. Then we developed a game plan.

"I prefer to teach someone to fish than to just do it for them, so we can start updating your site this week, if you want. It shouldn't take too long. You will need to compile a file of photos of your paintings, provide a bio, etcetera. Once you pull that all together, I can show you how to plug and play."

"Amazing. You are fantastic at this technical stuff."

"To me, it is just like building a house."

***

After Steve left, I jumped into the shower then called Hendrix.

"Hi."

"Hi, missed you today."

"Sorry, I got into a painting mood and didn't look up until dinner."

"What did the chef cook tonight?"

"Ha! Actually, I had Chinese. Steve brought some over."

"Steve?"

"Yes, Steve the carpenter. He helped me build the studio."

"That was nice of him."

"Unexpected. He offered to help me update my website."

"Wow, jack of all trades."

"Funny, I said the same thing."

There was a long pause. Finally, Hendrix asked, "Evie, is he interested in you?"

"No." I hoped my tone was convincing. To give Hendrix more comfort, I added, "We are just friends. Remember, Granddad helped him out, so I think he feels the need to look after me."

Sounding unconvinced, Hendrix responded, "Oh, right."

To change the subject, I asked, "How is Aja?"

"She is amazing. Guess what she asked me today."

"What?"

"When does she get to see you again?"

"Oh, that is so sweet. We can video conference anytime you would like."

"I was thinking something more personal. Why don't you come out for a visit?"

"Really?"

"Yes, really. I miss you, and your last visit … we both were in a different mindset."

"Are we ready for this again? Don't get me wrong, I would love to see you, but if we are taking it slow, a visit may not be the best next step."

"I think we can discuss the taking it slow when you are out here. I can get some time off in a couple of weeks. Can you come out then?"

"Hmm … Let me check with my social secretary." I paused for dramatic effect. "She said she will move some things," I replied jokingly.

"Wonderful! I can't wait to see you in the flesh."

"I can't wait to be seen in the flesh. I mean …" My face went bright red. "I mean, I can't wait to see you, as well."

"Good night, beautiful."

"Good night, Hendrix."

***

Over the next couple of days, I worked on getting the information ready for my website. The last and most difficult piece was my bio. Words just weren't coming to me, so I reached out to Tatum to see if she could help.

"Remember the day that we first met, and I asked you to tell me about yourself?"

"Yes."

"Well, this is the same process. I didn't want to know about your education or your jobs. I wanted to know about *you*. You the person, not the resume. Start there, and I'm sure you will come up with something fantastic."

"Tatum, you have more confidence in me than I do."

"We all have a unique and interesting story. You just have to be brave enough to tell it."

With that encouragement, I sat down at the kitchen table, laptop open, surrounded by little pieces of paper with notes written all over them. I closed my eyes and asked my higher self for some guidance. Then, after a few clearing breaths, I typed.

Evie Prince is not a technically trained artist. Her skills were learned from her grandmother, who was a well-known Martha's Vineyard landscape artist.

After her first attempt did not pay the bills, she moved into the world of corporate sales and marketing. Many years and a lot of soul searching later, Evie took a leap of faith and has once again embarked on a painting career. This time, however, she is on a journey, guided by the light in her heart.

Her art is an expansion of self and mind, emotional and thought-provoking. Evie Prince seeks truth of self through her art.

Wow, where had that come from? It sounded pretty good.

I grabbed my phone and texted Steve, letting him know I had all the information together and asked when we could work on the site.

He responded, *"I'm good for tomorrow night, if you are."*

"Sounds great. I will make dinner."

He responded with a thumbs-up.

CHAPTER 16 — COME TO LIFE

When I hit the button to book my flight, a wonderful surge of energy ran through my body. Then, to prepare for taking some time off, I took pictures of the pieces that Tatum would promote. The windows in the studio provided a wonderful, warm light that illuminated the paintings beautifully.

I heard Granddad's footsteps crunching up the walkway.

Before he knocked, I said, "Come on in."

"Not bad."

"I am learning from the best."

"Wow, look at all of your pieces. You have been busy."

"Taking photos so that, when I go back to Denver next week, my agent can start selling."

"Denver, huh? I guess things are back on with Hendrix."

"Well, we were on pause. He asked me to come out so we could talk about it. Plus, Aja would like to meet me."

"Huh, meeting the children is a big step. Well, I guess my next question is moot now."

"Why? What was it?"

"Not that it's any of my business, but Steve is very smitten with you. Seems like you two have been spending some time together."

"Yes, we have. He offered to help me update my website. Why would you say that?"

"Oh, I saw him over at the firehouse, and he mentioned you more than once. I know the look that he had in his eyes each time he said your name. He likes you. Have you told him about Hendrix?"

"No, there was no need to. First, I thought we were friends; and second, Hendrix and I were on hold. He hasn't asked, so …"

"Remember a few weeks ago when you almost ran over that mouse?"

"Yes."

"It may be time to think about the message."

"*Ugh*. How did this happen?"

"Why are you surprised? Evie, you are a beautiful woman with a big heart. Anyone would be attracted to you."

"Thank you, but I mean, I didn't ask for this. I didn't create this. How could it happen?"

"Think long and hard about that one. Things just don't happen. Remember, manifestation works in both directions. You create what you focus on. The Universe does not know the difference between not wanting and wanting something. It is the focus on the something that you manifest."

"Now what do I do?"

"You don't have to do anything. Give yourself some grace and ask for guidance. You'll know what you need to do when the time is right."

***

That evening, I wrapped myself in a blanket and sat outside on the deck. Seeing the stars and the light from the lighthouse gave me peace.

As I entered my mediation, I heard, "*What do you desire, Evie?*"

"I desire a partner in this physical life. Someone who I choose to love and who chooses to love me. A person who is supportive of me and my journey but is brave enough to be on their own journey. I desire someone who understands the importance of loving oneself and who wants to share their light with the world."

"*Then focus on that. Focus on what you desire, and it will come.*"

When I opened my eyes, I realized how far I had come on this journey. If someone had asked me that same question back in Denver, I would have given physical features, net worth, and age. None of that mattered now. I was stronger. There was no rush. When the time was right, then I would be ready.

***

"Hello?"

"Hi, Evie. It's Tatum. Wanted to let you know the site looks great, and I love your bio. I'll give it a big shout out in my next client communication."

"Thanks, Tatum. I had a good friend help me design it. The bio took some time, but it finally came together. Hey, I wanted to let you know I will be in town next week. Would be great to grab a coffee."

"Of course. Just let me know when you have time."

"Will do."

"Evie, I …" Tatum paused.

"Yes?"

"I was going to save this until it was more definite, but I can't keep it to myself any longer. There may be an opportunity through a local Bali tourism publication for an interview. Your commission piece is a tremendous hit at the hotel, and they would like to know more about you and the painting. Still trying to nail this down, but I wanted to at least let you know what I am working on."

"Really? That is amazing. Thank you."

"I am only the facilitator. It is your work that is getting all the attention. Enjoy it."

"I will. Thank you."

When I put the phone down, a slight smile crossed my face. *Thank you, Universe.* Things were really coming together.

I sent a note to Steve, thanking him again for his help with the website. He was quick to respond.

"Glad everything worked out. Next week, there is a local band playing down island, and I was wondering if you would like to go."

I am not ready for this, I thought to myself. What should I say? It took me a few minutes to reply.

"Oh no. That sounds like a great time, but unfortunately, I can't. I am heading to Colorado next week for a break."

"Really? Going to do some skiing?"

"Actually, visiting a special friend and his daughter."

It took him longer than usual to respond.

"Oh, cool. Well, have a great time."

"Thanks, and thank you again for all of your help."

"Anytime."

Why did I feel so crappy from that exchange? I felt like I was hiding something, but there was nothing to hide. I was never good at relationship stuff. Nuances, reading into things—I disliked it all. Now here I was, back in it.

The Steve conversation weighed heavily on me. I could not release the uneasy feeling. Therefore, when I called Colbie to let her know I would be in town, I told her about it.

"So, I feel like I'm hiding something from Steve."

"Do you believe you owe him something? Has he said that he likes you?"

"Yes and no. Yes, I feel like I owe him, because he has been so generous to me; and no, he has not told me."

"So, is this more you than him?"

"I don't know."

"Evie, you do not owe him anything. He was generous with his time and expertise. When you taught him how to paint, were you expecting anything from him?"

"No, I wanted to share the gift that my grandmother gave to me."

"Exactly. So why do you think he expects something from you?"

"Because someone always wants something."

"Wow, that is a hell of a belief."

"I know."

"Do you like how that belief feels?"

"No, not at all."

"So, what do you need to do?"

"Change that belief."

"Exactly. What belief would make you feel better?"

"That people do because they want to, and they expect nothing in return."

"Is that what you do?"

"Yes, for the most part."

"Well then, know that others can do it, as well."

"I hear ya. Thanks."

"Just out of curiosity, have you ever thought about Steve as more than just a friend? Are you attracted to him?"

"He is cute, has a good heart, and is generous. He has supported me since I moved to the island and knows I am on a journey and is not afraid to be open about his own. Through all this, he is learning to love himself. Just like I am learning to love me."

"Are these attributes that you want in a partner?"

At that moment, I realized Steve was exactly what I asked my higher self for in a partner.

"Yes, they are."

"Well then, maybe you should give him a chance."

"But I am coming out to see Hendrix."

"And ...?"

"And we are going to talk about us."

"Good. Don't think too far ahead of yourself. Live in the moment and enjoy your life. Continue to ask for guidance, and you will know what to do when the time comes."

I released a huge sigh. "Colbie, you are good. You always help me find clarity."

"Happy to help. Call me if you have any free time when you are out here."

"Will do."

Colbie had a point. I needed to live in the present, but for some reason the beach dream popped into my head. Was the man I was holding hands with on the beach Hendrix or was it someone else? Could it be Steve? It was all too much to think about. I had to trust that it will be revealed when it was time.

For the rest of the week, I cleaned, packed, and moved all my paintings into the spare room. Before I closed the door, I looked at what I had created and felt at peace.

Grandmother, thank you for this gift. I just wish you could have been free with your art when you were on earth.

In the back of my mind, I heard a whisper. *"I chose my life. You have chosen yours. Enjoy this gift and share it with the world."*

***

Granddad took me to the boat, and the Peter Pan bus chauffeured me to Logan airport. My flight was direct to Denver so, in a few brief hours, I would back in Colorado.

As we taxied into the gate, I texted Hendrix, letting him know that we had just landed. Then I grabbed some gum and slipped it under my mask. I never knew what type of greeting I would receive, so better to be safe than sorry.

The train from gate to baggage claim was busy. We poured out of the cars at the last stop, and everyone was jockeying to get on the escalator. People filled the receiving area.

Before I stepped off the escalator, I took a quick scan of the crowd. Right in front, with a big sign saying, *"Welcome Evie,"* was Aja, jumping up and down.

"Daddy, Daddy, she's here. Evie is here."

I dropped my bags and knelt down. She ran right over to me.

"Hi, Evie. I'm Aja."

"Hi, Aja. It is so nice to see you in person. May I have a hug?"

"Yup!" And she threw her arms around my neck.

"Aja, you are a great hugger. Big, warm hugs just how I like them."

"Daddy gives big, warm hugs, too."

"I know." I looked up, and there was Hendrix with his beautiful smile looking down at me. He grabbed my hand and helped me up.

"May I have a hug?"

"Yes, of course."

His arms enveloped me in a familiar but electrified embrace. He felt so good that I didn't want to let go. Finally, we noticed Aja jumping up and down again.

"Me, too! Me, too!"

Hendrix picked her up, and then we had a magnificent hug.

"So, how was your flight?"

"Great. Slept most of the way."

"Is this all your stuff?"

"Yes, I packed light."

Hendrix put Aja down then grabbed my bags. Aja grabbed my hand, and we walked out to the car.

"I figured we can grab something to eat, and then I'll take Aja back to her mom's when she gets home from work."

"Perfect."

***

Hendrix had definitely upgraded his home. It was no longer a bachelor pad. The living room furniture worked perfectly in his space, and my painting was front and center.

"I love what you've done to the place."

He smiled. "Yes, I grew up a bit. Aja needs a place she can call home and, for the first time, I felt like I needed to create a home, for her and for me."

"I bet Nik is proud."

"She is never satisfied. Now she thinks I'm an old man."

I laughed. "Boy, she knows how to push your buttons."

He chuckled. "I guess she does."

When Hendrix returned from dropping off Aja, I could tell we both felt uncomfortable. It was easy when Aja was around, because we didn't have to think about the elephant in the room, but now that she was gone, how would we act?

"I feel our greeting was interrupted at the airport by a cute three-year-old wanting in on the hug. Can we do that greeting again?"

When I smiled, Hendrix pulled me in for a wonderfully deep, long hug. I had missed his smell.

He looked down at me with those eyes, and I knew I was in trouble. His energy pulsed through me, and then he slowly and gently kissed my lips.

"Thank you for making the trip. I really missed you."

When I opened my eyes, he was smiling at me. I blushed. "Thank you for the invitation."

He walked me over to the couch and sat me down. "What would you like to do while you're here? I have some surprises, but this was your town, too."

"It may sound silly, but I would like to see Denver and Colorado as a tourist. There was so much that I took for granted while I lived here. I would like to really see and feel it."

"Done."

The calendar almost said spring, but Colorado had its own seasons. For every excursion, we dressed in layers, not knowing what to expect. The sun and Hendrix did not disappoint. We had beautiful weather everywhere we went—Estes Park, Boulder, and the Rocky Mountain National Park. We drove out to Garden of the Gods and Pikes Peak, drank beer, went to the art museum, and even toured the Denver Mint. In-between all that, we played house and spent a lot of quality time getting reacquainted with each other. Not only did I love this man, but I was also in love with him. Everything just felt so right when we were together. Having Aja with us made it complete. I couldn't remember ever being this happy.

A couple of afternoons, Hendrix had to work, so I took the opportunity to see Tatum and Colbie. It was wonderful spending time with those ladies. Both of them had this amazing presence. They helped me think, settled my mind, and gave me peace.

"So, how is it going with Hendrix?" Colbie coyly asked.

"We are having a fantastic time. It differs from the first time we got together. The attraction is still there, but somehow it is even more and in a different way. I love just talking to him, learning about him. We feed off of each other. And, dare I say, make each other better."

"Well, I'm happy for you. You deserve all the happiness in the world."

"Thank you. I am ashamed to say that, even with all this happiness, as the days pass, I feel some anxiety."

"About what?"

"I don't want to leave him, but my home is back East now. He can't leave because of Aja. How could this possibly work?"

"Evie, breathe. It is possible. You are having limiting thoughts. Please stay open and enjoy this moment. If you bring worry, you will miss all the beauty. If this is meant to be, it will be. You never know what the future holds, so stay positive and have fun."

I closed my eyes and took some deep breaths. "You're right. Why ruin this amazing time with worry? I am open and allowing the wonderful things that this life has in store for me."

***

Tatum and I met for coffee at our usual spot. She looked great, as always, and made me feel like I was her only artist.

"Evie, you look fantastic. Your eyes are sparkling. Is there something that you want to tell me?"

"This has been a wonderful trip, and I am so happy."

"I can tell, and I'm so glad to hear that. You are a completely different woman than when we first met. Your confidence just radiates off of you."

"Thank you. I have done a lot of growing. Let go of many things that were holding me back and found some new things that help me stay open and positive."

"Wonderful. Well, your paintings are as exquisite as ever. Brighter, but still filled with emotion. I don't feel I will have any problem selling your new pieces."

"I love the sound of that. Any word on the interview?"

"Not yet, but we are moving in a positive direction."

Before we left, Tatum mentioned something about an artist tour overseas but wouldn't give me more details until she had some definite information to share.

"Stay tuned, Evie, and keep up the amazing work."

"Thanks. I'll call you when I get back to the island."

On the way back to Hendrix's house, I stopped by my favorite Poke place and picked up two bowls. Then, when I got back, I put a blanket down on the living room floor and set it with plastic ware.

When Hendrix walked into the house, he just laughed. "What a beautiful memory. Our first date. Now look at us."

"So glad that you remembered."

"How could I forget? That night changed my life."

***

The next morning, we slept in and enjoyed each other's company. However, there was a weight in the room. I was scheduled to leave tomorrow, so this would be our last full day together.

"Why don't we take a hike and get some fresh air?" Hendrix suggested.

"Yes, I feel the need to be out in the mountain air."

There was a short hike just outside of Boulder. It took no time to get there. The air was brisk. Blue sky, white clouds, and a mountain backdrop. It all was spectacular.

We sat in silence at the top of the overlook, taking in the beauty. We held hands, and I could feel the energy running through us.

Hendrix pulled me close and put his arm around me. "Amazing, isn't it?"

"Yes, this view is spectacular."

Hendrix turned to look at me. "Evie, thank you for making the trip out to see us. Aja just loves being with you. She feeds off your energy and comes to life when she's with you."

"Aja is a very special little girl. She is filled with light."

"I also come to life when I am with you." Hendrix looked at me with his deep brown eyes. "Evie, you make me happy. Your light fills me with joy and peace. I want to make a life with you. Please stay and marry me?"

My heart raced and my mind went blank. Then I closed my eyes and quietly wept.

Evie's story continues…

REFERENCES

Gay Head Lighthouse. www.gayheadlight.org
Jamie Sams & David Carson. *Medicine Cards*. St. Martin's Press, 1999

CHAPTER 1 — LEAP OF FAITH

It seemed like forever before I could say a word, as thoughts raced through my mind. I loved him, but what about my new life on Martha's Vineyard? What about Aja? Could he leave her, or did he have to stay in Colorado?

I wiped the tears from my eyes as Hendrix gazed down at me, his eyes filled with love. Not expecting me to hesitate before answering his marriage proposal, his face then turned from love to concern.

"Evie, are you okay? Is there something wrong?"

"I didn't think I would ever hear those words said to me. I want to say yes, but …"

"But what?"

I lowered my head. "I am scared."

"Scared of what?"

"Hendrix, I love you, but can this work? Now that Aja is in your life, you need to be with her. She is so young and needs a full-time father. I enjoy my new life on the island and being near my granddad. I don't want to move back to Colorado. How can this possibly work?" I asked, my eyes filled with tears.

"Evie, slow down and breathe." He watched me take a few deep breaths. "Do you want to spend your life with me?"

"Of course."

"Well, then we can figure this out."

"But, how?" I asked, my voice filled with apprehension.

"Do you believe we can create the life we desire?"

"Yes, you know I do."

"Then we will create the life we desire." Hendrix took my hand in his. "Evie Prince, will you marry me?"

I looked deep into his soulful eyes and took a deep breath. "Hendrix Talisman, yes, I will marry you."

***

I felt like I floated the entire hike back to the car. Our smiles and the love that we felt for each other created an energy that even strangers felt. We had an intimate dinner at a fantastic little noodle shop to celebrate. I smiled so much my face hurt. Then, that night, as we lay in bed, I turned to Hendrix.

"We can figure this out, right?"

"Evie, please do not worry. We will make this work. Stay open to all the possibilities." From under his pillow, he pulled out a simple yet stunning emerald ring, flanked by a diamond on each side, and slipped it on my finger. "Evie, this ring represents the love that I share with you."

The brilliance of the ring took my breath away. "Hendrix, this is absolutely beautiful."

"To me, you symbolize the emerald. The stone of successful love, it opens the heart and nurtures the heart chakra. It embodies compassion, unity, and unconditional love. That is what you and your energy give to me." He then kissed me, and we fell into oneness.

***

My week in Colorado had come to an end. At the airport, my heart was heavy at leaving Hendrix, but we were committed to each other, and, in time, we would live our lives together.

As the plane climbed higher in the sky, I looked at the Denver landscape. So much had changed, including me, but could I live here again? The thought was too much for me to handle. I looked at my ring, smiled, and then closed my eyes and fell asleep.

When Granddad picked me up at the boat, I felt like a walking zombie. Going to a destination always seemed easier than coming back.

Granddad welcomed me with an enormous hug. "Hey, kid. How was your trip?"

"Amazing."

"I can tell you're tired, but I can see a sparkle in your eyes. Everything work out with you two?"

I held up my left hand and smiled.

"Whoa. Seems like it worked out better than expected." He chuckled. "Congratulations."

"Thank you."

We walked to Granddad's truck, and I put my bag in the back. The drive up island gave me peace. I glanced over at Granddad and could tell he was thinking.

"So, is this something that would happen soon, or …?"

"No, we still have things to work out, but we know we want to spend our lives together. We just have to figure out how we can do it."

"Is he willing to move here?"

"Before finding out about his daughter, I would have said yes. But now, who knows? Aja is only three years old, and she needs him, and I know he cannot live without her. So, there lies the dilemma."

We were both silent until we pulled into my road. Then Granddad hesitantly asked, "Would you move back to Colorado?"

"I don't know. My life here on the island and being with you has been amazing. I can't imagine not being here."

"Well, just stay open, and I am sure you both will create the life that you want to live together."

I smiled. "That's exactly what Hendrix said."

ABOUT THE AUTHOR

Inspirational writer, Victoria Wright, has embarked on a journey to find her true self. In the process, she is remembering how to be whole, to look inward for guidance, and to know her truth. Her journey is full of beauty and discovery. She invites you to embark on your own journey of remembering.

Victoria is from Martha's Vineyard, Massachusetts and is a member of the Wampanoag Tribe of Gay Head Aquinnah. Currently, she and her family reside just outside of Denver, Colorado.